ALL DUE RESPECT 2021

CHRIS RHATIGAN &
DAVID NEMETH, EDITORS

ALL DUE RESPECT 2021

All Due Respect Books
an imprint of Down & Out Books
3959 Van Dyke Road, Suite 265
Lutz, FL 33558
DownAndOutBooks.com

The characters and events in this book are fictitious. Any similarity
to real persons, living or dead, is coincidental and not intended by
the author.

Cover design by JT Lindroos

ISBN: 1-64396-264-7
ISBN-13: 978-1-64396-264-1

TABLE OF CONTENTS

A Brave Man

By John Rector

I needed money, so I took a job working the door at the Glass Tiger, a mid-scale burlesque club down by the water. It was a nice enough place. The dancers were young, and the bartenders wore bowties and served drinks under neon lights.

My job was to check IDs and explain the rules. There was a long list, but I summed them up in three words:

Mind your manners.

Occasionally someone would forget those three words and that's when I'd step in.

Usually they left quietly.

If they didn't, I'd make them bleed.

One night, Kristi, one of the new girls, stopped to talk.

"How do you do it?" she asked. "You never lose your cool."

I told her I didn't take anything personally.

She laughed, kissed my cheek, and said, "I'd hate to see what would happen if you did." She reached up and wiped her lipstick from my cheek with her thumb, and then disappeared into the club.

I thought about that kiss for a long time.

From then on, Kristi would talk to me every night. She told me she lived with her boyfriend across town. I saw him pick her up after her shifts, but he never went inside.

When I asked why he never watched her work, she looked at me like I'd said something wrong.

"Sorry," I said. "It's not my business."

"It's okay." She did her best to smile. "He doesn't like what I do."

If I were a brave man, I would've told her that if she were mine, I would watch her on stage every night, overflowing with pride.

But I wasn't a brave man, and I never said a word.

* * *

The first time Kristi didn't show up for her shift, I didn't think much of it. When she missed three shifts, I started to worry. If she missed another, Karl would take her off the schedule. But it never came to that, because on the fourth night she was there.

The bruises hadn't quite faded.

When her shift ended, she stopped to talk.

I asked if she was okay.

"Fine." She tried to say more, but there were only tears.

I asked if she wanted me to talk to him.

"Please don't."

I nodded and told her to go wash her face.

While she was inside, her boyfriend pulled up and held his hand on the horn.

I approached the car. "She'll be out when she's out."

I went back to my spot by the door and watched him park. He got out and crossed the lot toward the stairs and tried to push past me.

I put a hand on his chest and said, "Ten dollars."

"I'm just going to—"

"Ten dollars."

He knocked my hand away, considered me, then wisely reached for his wallet.

I took the money and said, "Mind your manners."

When the commotion started, I went in just in time to see him pulling Kristi toward the door. I almost stepped in, but then I saw the look on her face. I barely recognized her. The light in her eyes was gone, replaced by fear and shame.

I let them pass, but I followed them to the parking lot.

When they reached his car, he pushed her away and turned on me.

"Something you want to say, motherfucker?"

I said, "Leave her alone."

He came closer, and I was ready for him.

Then Kristi yelled, "No!"

I looked at her, distracted, and didn't see the flash of metal in his hand until I felt the blade bury itself in my side, just above my waist.

It didn't hurt, at least not until I grabbed his hand and pulled it away. Once the blade was out, I twisted his arm hard, snapping the bones from his elbow to his wrist.

He screamed, and the knife hit the ground.

I felt the blood run down my side, and the world around me turned red. I stepped in, grabbed the back of

3

his head, and slammed his face into the doorframe of his car, over and over again.

Far away, Kristi was begging me to stop, but by the time her voice cut through the haze, it was too late. I felt his skull give with the last hit, and his body went limp.

I let him fall.

Kristi pushed past me and knelt over him. She reached for him, but when she saw his face she pulled away, put her hands to her mouth, and began to scream.

I went back to the door, sat on my stool, and looked down at my side. The blood was flowing freely, and I pressed my hand against the wound, wincing.

One of the girls said, "I called an ambulance."

"Thank you."

"The cops too," she said. "You might want to leave."

I didn't understand, and I was about to ask her why when Kristi turned and started screaming at me.

"You!" She pointed at me, her hands red with his blood. "Look what you've done! You're a fucking animal! A fucking animal!"

The words stung, and I felt a lump form in my throat. My eyes were wet, and I looked down at the blood dripping on the ground beneath me, hiding my face so she wouldn't see.

Kristi was still crying when the cops arrived, but I didn't look at her again until the paramedics strapped me onto the stretcher and loaded me into the back of the ambulance.

The last time I saw her, she looked broken.

I closed my eyes, heard the doors slam, and felt the ambulance pull away.

That final image of Kristi was seared into my brain, but I tried to hold on to how she looked before, standing alone on stage, swaying like a goddess beneath a crystal rainbow of light, while a congregation of the unworthy worshipped at her feet.

If only I could've told her.

If only she would've known.

If only I were a brave man.

John Rector is the bestselling author of the novels The Grove, The Cold Kiss, Already Gone, Out of the Black, Ruthless, The Ridge, *and* Broken. *His books have been translated into over 20 languages, and his short fiction has appeared in numerous magazines and won several awards including the International Thriller Award for his novella* Lost Things.

He lives in Omaha, Nebraska.

Lottery Tickets and Cigarettes

By Stephen D. Rogers

Brad placed his energy drink on the counter and turned to Kyle, who'd only started yesterday, much too new to really form a judgment. "You want anything?"

Kyle sniffed. "Nah, I'm good. We don't get paid until Friday anyway."

"I'll cover if you want something." The nice thing about working for Handy Dandy—probably the only part of the job that didn't suck—was getting paid in cash. "You want one of these, a soda, maybe some gum? They got donuts there in the case."

Kyle wiped his nose with the back of his hand. "Ah...give me a lottery ticket."

The Indian woman behind the counter blinked. "Which one?"

"The winning one." Kyle guffawed, pounding Brad on the back hard enough to send him crashing against the counter.

Brad cleared his throat. "Make it a two-dollar scratch." While he didn't want to appear cheap, he didn't want to throw away his money either, just in case Kyle

7

"forgot" to pay back the loan.

The clerk repeated, more softly, "Which one?"

For the first time, Brad really noticed the plastic bins taking up half the wall behind the counter, the scratch tickets tagged with prices ranging from one to thirty. Thirty dollars for a scratch ticket? Who bought these things?

Kyle slapped the counter. "Fuck this." Reaching under the T-shirt emblazoned with "Handy Dandy— No Job Too Ugly," he pulled out a gun. "Just give me a whole bunch of them."

Brad stepped back, his hands splayed. "Whoa. What are you doing?"

The barrel wavered as Kyle enunciated, "I am trying my luck with the state lottery."

"Kyle, put away the gun. I told you, I got this covered. Think of it as a gift. Welcome to the job. It's good to have you on the team." What the hell was wrong with this guy?

The Indian woman yanked a ribbon of tickets out of the nearest bin and pulled sideways to tear them off. "Take them. Just go."

She tossed the snarl of tickets onto the counter and stepped back, tripping over something on the floor and maintaining her balance only by throwing an arm up against the plastic bins.

Bang. Her metal bracelets.

Kyle winked at Brad before pointing the gun at her head. "None of those look like winners. You saying I look like a loser? That my friend here looks like a loser?"

"Kyle...We're...we're going to be late."

Was that really the best he could come up?

The clerk pulled streamers of tickets from two different

bins. "Here." She held them out to Kyle as if it was an offering.

Kyle turned to Brad. "Are you just going to stand there gawking, or are you going to take them from the lady? My hand is sort of busy holding the gun."

"Forget the tickets. Let's just go."

"What, you think she can just slip them back inside their little glass cages? That's not how it works. Brad, she tore them off."

"So what?"

"Those tickets are ours. Fifty-fifty, you and me."

"I want no part."

Kyle laughed. "No part? You wanted to drive the truck, boss. That makes you the getaway driver on this here heist."

Brad shook his head, searching for a way to de-escalate this mess. "We should just leave. If we go right now, I'm sure we can all forget this even happened." He pleaded with the clerk, "That okay with you?"

The Indian woman nodded.

Kyle frowned. "Brad, take the fucking tickets."

A five-tone melody announced somebody else had entered the store.

Brad turned to see a cop lifting a newspaper from the pile, and almost ran over to give him a hug. Everything would be—

Bam, bam, bam.

The cop's throat exploded with a spray of red, and his head just…

A crash as the cop tumbled back against the door, the weight of his body pushing it open.

Brad's heart stopped. His hands, pressed against his ears, made him think of seashells on the beach, echoes of the waves, endless days leaving footprints in the wet sand.

"Woo-eee!" Kyle blew across the end of the upturned barrel. "We are having some fun now."

Brad stared at his coworker, recalling that not so long ago Brad had thought he didn't know the guy well enough to judge.

Kyle leaned across the counter and pointed his gun down at the woman wailing out of sight. "Shut the fuck up!"

The clerk struggled to choke the wailing to a whimper.

Brad forced his hands from his ears. "What did you do?"

"Aimed where he wasn't wearing a vest, that's what I did."

Hearing the five-tone melody, Brad spun expecting to see a second chance. Instead, he saw the door propped open by the dead cop.

Dead. Brad had never seen a dead person. Never seen actual violence acted out in the real world. This just didn't make any sense.

Bing, bong. Bing, bong, bing.

Kyle tucked the gun in the back of his pants. "Help me pull him inside."

Brad searched for the words. "You shot him. Why did you shoot him? Why would you shoot a cop?"

"I guess you could say I was resisting arrest."

Bing, bong. Bing, bong, bing.

Kyle grabbed an ankle with each hand and lifted. "You want to help or just stand there and watch?"

"I don't believe this." Brad paced in front of counter.

"This guy's not light. Just saying."

"I stopped to get an energy drink. Asked if you wanted

to come in with me; that was a mistake. I went for my wallet, and you went for a gun."

Kyle dragged the body down the middle aisle and yelled, "Any time you want to step in and lend a hand, that would be great. Maybe if you're feeling peckish, you could crack open that energy drink that was so damn important."

For a second, Brad considered heading out the door. Even if he made it outside, even if he got in the truck and drove away, what difference would it make?

"Kyle, you killed someone. Right here in front of me. Who even brings a gun to work?"

"Cops for one." A double-tap of boot heels hitting the floor. "You want his?"

"No, I don't want his gun. I don't want any gun. I need to think." Brad covered his face. "We're in so much trouble. What are we going to do?"

"I've changed my mind. I think I will have a donut."

"We should be at work right now, Kyle, carting trash out of some shithole."

"You didn't want to go to work." Kyle bit off half the cruller, chewed twice, and swallowed. "I could tell. You were just going through the motions."

"You're insane."

"Maybe a cigarette would help you calm the fuck down."

"I don't smoke."

Kyle stuffed the rest of the cruller into his mouth and leaned over the counter, crumbs flying as he said, "My friend here needs to start smoking."

A carton arced up to land on the counter.

"I'll assume that service came with a smile. It was funny, anyway." Kyle presented the carton to Brad.

"Don't say I never gave you anything."

Brad brushed the carton aside. "You do know what you did, right? You killed somebody."

"Only if he dies. If he doesn't die, it's just attempted murder, maybe assault with a deadly weapon. Shit, if the judge is soft-hearted, maybe I can plea to disturbing the peace."

Brad pointed at the aisle. "Did that cop look like he just wanted to rest a minute before he got up to go about his business?"

"Can't say that he did." Kyle shook his head. "No, I'll give long odds that he's a goner."

"We are so fucked."

"Brad. If you're not going to use those smokes, maybe we could return them for store credit."

"How can you make jokes?"

"I hear ya, Brad. I hear the disappointment in your voice. You're thinking: I can't become friends with someone like him. I think he might have a gambling problem."

Kyle reached for a clump of scratch tickets and dragged them closer. "You know, I think you might be right."

He pulled the gun from the rear of his pants and used the edge of the grip to scratch at the silver circles. "I like to skip to the results. Then I go back to see what I'm trying to match."

Talking to Kyle was pointless. "I'm going to call the police."

"No, you're not."

Brad nodded. "I don't know how, but I'm going to try to explain this."

"It's too late, Brad."

"Why?"

"Brad. Is that short for Bradley?"

"Bradford. It was my grandfather's name."

"You ever meet him?"

Brad shook his head. "Forget my grandfather. Why is it too late to call the police?"

Kyle placed his gun on the counter, separated one ticket from the rest, and blew away the silver dust. "Five bucks." He showed the winning ticket to Brad.

"Great. Wonderful."

Kyle leaned over the counter. "You hear that? You owe me five bucks."

"Kyle, why is it too late to call the cops?"

"The clerk on the floor already did. I heard her press three buttons while you were cleaning wax out of your ears. Seriously, you didn't hear her muffling the phone when dispatch tried to get more information?"

"They can track the phone. They'll send help."

Kyle spun away in laughter. "Help? You think anybody is going to send us help? Brad, we are the outlaws. That means we are outside the law." Kyle removed another donut from the case. "Nobody comes to save the likes of you and me. We are on our own."

Brad leapt forward and grabbed the gun off the counter. He took two large steps back, raised the gun with shaking hands, and pointed at Kyle. "I'm in charge now."

"Good. I was tired of doing all the heavy lifting." Kyle took a large bite of the sugar frosted. "What's the plan, boss?"

Powdered sugar covered Kyle's T-shirt.

"You are going to stay here."

"Not leaving until I get my five bucks."

Brad backed toward the door. "When the police arrive, I'm going to tell them what happened."

"I hear they're good listeners."

"No, wait. She comes with me. Hey, you, behind the counter. We're leaving."

Kyle turned toward the counter. "Before you go, you owe me some money."

Brad heard the clerk scramble.

A hand reached up and tapped buttons on the register until the drawer opened. "Take everything."

Kyle walked over to the counter, peered inside the drawer, and plucked out a five. "We're good. You can go."

The clerk scurried from behind the counter. Stopped rather than pass too close to Kyle.

He raised his hands and backed two steps down an aisle.

Trying to block the memory of the dead officer, the sight of his throat exploding, Brad motioned the Indian woman should run to him, which she did.

Brad raised his voice. "Kyle? You just stay put. I'll tell them you're unarmed. I'll tell them...things got out of hand, that you didn't mean to hurt anybody. Kyle?"

Brad heard the clerk push through the door to freedom, to what remained of normalcy.

Bing, bong. Bing, bong, bing.

"Kyle, I'm leaving now. Everything's going to be okay."

Sirens in the distance. The cavalry.

Brad took a step backwards. Another. "Kyle?"

"What?" Kyle stepped around the end of an aisle, a gun in his hand. "Sorry it took me so long, boss, but I had a hell of a time with his holster. Thanks for holding down the fort."

"Put it on the counter."

In one fluid movement, Kyle raised the gun until it was pointed to the left of Brad and fired three shots. "Get down, it's the cops!"

Brad scurried away from the large windows and vaulted over the counter. There was no way he wanted to be between Kyle and the cops.

A loudspeaker crackled. "This is the police. Come out with your hands up. I want to see empty hands. Come out and lay down on the ground, arms out straight like they're wings on a bird."

Unable to shake the urge to know what was happening, Brad shifted into a crouch so he could see over the counter.

Kyle strode into the center of the store with a large bag of ice. Grinning, he swung the bag and let go, the ice crashing through the window where he'd placed three shots.

He yelled, "We have hostages in here. A pregnant woman and her little boy."

A beat of silence. "Do you have a cell phone?"

"There are some pay-as-you-go phones new in their packages. Do you think I can activate one without going online? Fuck you!"

Chuckling, Kyle returned to the aisles.

Brad dropped until he sat on his heels. Kyle was going to get them killed. Kyle would probably shoot Brad if he made a run for the door. That's if the cops didn't shoot him first.

Was it so much to ask, sipping from an energy drink on the way to the job? Driving a coworker who wasn't batshit crazy?

Kyle shot that cop. Killed him. No reason at all.

Brad covered his eyes.

The loudspeaker: "Does the pregnant woman have a cell phone?"

Kyle yelled, "Doesn't want a mutant fetus."

What the hell was wrong with Kyle?

Did Handy Dandy hire just anybody?

Brad slumped onto the floor, looking down the alley behind the counter. At the far end: a plain white door.

"Do Not Enter." "Employees Only." "No Smoking."

There was probably an office on the other side. Maybe an emergency exit. Maybe just a window. If Brad could get into the office, he could shove something against the door to keep Kyle from following. A desk. A table. A chair under the doorknob, however that was supposed to work.

If there was an office, there had to be phone. He'd call the police and explain the situation. There was no pregnant woman with her little boy. Brad was the hostage. Kyle was armed with the cop's gun; Kyle was insane.

Unless the door was locked. Of course it was locked. What was Brad going to do, stand there slamming his shoulder against the door while Kyle sauntered over to shoot Brad in the back of the head?

Fuck.

Brad looked away from the door, lowered his gaze, noticed Kyle's gun still clutched in his hands.

He didn't know anything about firing a gun. Didn't even know if he was holding it correctly.

What the hell was he supposed to do, shoot his way out? Challenge Kyle to a duel? Fire at the doorknob as if that wouldn't fuck up the lock?

Brad shielded his eyes from the fluorescent lights.

16

"Kyle, you still there?"

"No way. Once I won the lottery, I gave my notice and went to Hawaii. Fuck Handy Dandy."

"I'm looking at an office door. There's got to be a second exit. It's fire code."

"You don't think there's cops out back?"

Fuck. Brad hadn't considered that possibility.

"Why'd you say the hostage was a pregnant woman? You could have said two guys. You could have made demands, and then when the cops asked you to send out the hostages first, we could have gone out with hands raised."

"You'd probably have to piss in your pants for them to buy it."

"Already took care of that."

"Ha! Hold tight, boss. We're in control of this situation. Cops got a bullhorn? Big fucking deal. We've got enough processed food to create a weapon of mass destruction."

"Why don't you yell that a little louder? Maybe they'll send in government assassins." Brad rubbed his eyes until he saw colored lights.

This was not his life. This was a nightmare. This was worse than a nightmare because there was no waking up.

"Yo, Brad."

"What?"

"Tell me the truth. You think we're going to get fired for not showing up on time?" Kyle chuckled.

Fucking lunatic.

Brad took a deep breath.

Maybe the key was to simply wait until Kyle got bored and rushed the door. Or the cops came in through the back.

They'd kick open the office door, see him sitting here with his hands up, piss running down his leg.

Kyle would do something stupid, and they'd engage him, forgetting for a moment Brad who was obviously no threat.

Brad would keep his hands raised, and they'd take him into custody. Ask him to explain what couldn't be explained.

"Yo, boss!"

"What?"

"I'm thinking I might cut a deal."

"Great idea." They probably couldn't wait to negotiate a lesser sentence for a cop killer. "You do that, Kyle."

"I figure, why not? It was your idea to come in here. You're the senior man. You're holding the gun that killed that cop. I mean...I got information they want to hear. I got no problem testifying."

"You have got to be fucking kidding me." Brad climbed to his feet. "All you had to do today was carry trash out of a shithole and leave it in bins by the side of the road. That's it." Brad marched down the alley behind the counter. "Is that what you did, Kyle?"

"Don't remember doing that."

"No. Apparently, that was too easy. Instead, you decided to rob a convenience store and kill a cop."

Brad raised the gun as he advanced into the first aisle. Empty.

He spun into the second aisle to see a streak of blood leading to that very cop. The breath went out of him.

"Yo, boss."

Brad looked up to see Kyle standing at the other side of the aisle, a cocky grin on his face. "Do we get a fifteen-minute break or what?"

Brad raised the gun and pulled the trigger as fast as he could.

Cops yelling at him to put down the weapon, raise his hands, lay on the ground.

Brad turned to explain, his arms going wide, gun still in his hand.

* * *

Shots were returned.

Stephen D. Rogers is the author of Shot to Death, *published by All Due Respect, and more than 800 shorter works. His website, StephenDRogers.com, includes a list of new and upcoming titles as well as other timely information.*

Any Deadly Thing

By Emily Bay Moore

Johannah was eleven the first time she took up snakes.

It was long as she was tall and the color of old pennies. It stank of ammonia. When Daddy opened its tank, Jo wanted to cover her nose. The zookeepers on Animal Planet picked up snakes just behind the head—so they couldn't snap back and bite—but Daddy said the whole point of taking up serpents was to put your faith in God to see you through. Taking precautions like that meant you were a coward and an atheist.

Jo held the snake two-handed. It was as soft and dry as the leather seats of her grandpa's Cadillac. It squirmed so hard Jo almost dropped it, which would have been worse than getting bit. The entire congregation was watching. Daddy's hands were heavy as cinder blocks on her shoulders.

She was glad when Daddy took it away. She got to sit down next to her sisters and try not to touch her face with dirty snake hands while her parents passed around a bottle of strychnine for the grown-ups to drink.

That night they had fried chicken for dinner. It was

Jo's favorite and Daddy said she'd done good, up on stage. Halloween only being a week away, but the kitchen was summertime hot. Every burner had a bubbling pot. Opening the oven could singe the peach fuzz off her cheeks.

Together, they were a conveyor belt. Ma fixed plates. Jo delivered them.

"Open this for me, Hannie-baby." Ma was struggling with a bag of chips. Her thumb was in a splint and she couldn't grip things right.

"Yes, ma'am." Jo stole a pickle chip so vinegary it burned her tongue. She poured the rest into a plastic bowl. It was University of Kentucky blue and white.

"Take those out to Daddy." Ma was hunched over the open oven, just where she liked to be. Ma was a hundred pounds wet. She loathed how cold Daddy kept it in the rest of the house. Maybe that's why she hung around the kitchen during family parties.

"Yes, ma'am."

Their kitchen table only seated four—not including the high chair for baby Sarah Lynn—and with the entire extended family over, there wasn't enough space. They ate in the living room. Adults got chairs. Little kids sat on the floor.

Today's service meant Jo didn't have to sit with the babies anymore. Daddy dragged out a rickety folding chair just for her. Too bad she was on her feet playing hostess the whole night. Her cousin Naplan stole the chair out from under her.

She dodged between chatting grown-ups without interrupting conversation. Good hostesses didn't bother their guests except to refill drinks. It didn't matter that she was supposed to be the guest of honor. At Ma's last birthday party, neither of them got a slice of cake.

She made it to Daddy's easy chair without spilling a single chip. He was talking with his brother, Jo's Uncle Emmett. She tried to covertly replace Daddy's empty bowl with her fresh one while they were both distracted arguing about John Calipari. She failed.

"Were you scared, Jo?" Emmett was smoking in the house again. Jo's parents hated it.

"Johannah," Daddy emphasized her Christian name, "didn't have any reason to be scared."

"C'mon, Lionel, you can't blame a little girl for being scared of snakes." Uncle Emmett ashed into what Jo hoped was an empty can of beer. Last Christmas he accidentally dropped a butt into Grandpa's dip spit bottle. The burnt smell made her gag.

"We prayed for forgiveness together before the service. As long as she had the Holy Spirit with her, everything would be fine. Mark 16:18, they will take up—"

"I know the scripture too. I dropped out of high school, but I can read. I was asking the girl."

Daddy's teeth clacked together. Uncle Emmett was cruel to wind Daddy up this way when he would never have to deal with the repercussions. It always fell back on Ma.

He better pray on that before next Sunday. God didn't protect the unrepentant.

"Jo?"

"I wasn't scared. I was happy that Daddy thought I was finally ready. We had a real great prayer session, just the two of us." They kneeled together in the preacher's office until her knees were printed with red bumps from the carpet.

Uncle Emmett hummed. "What's a sweet thing like

23

you got to say sorry for? Did you take your Daddy's car on a joyride? Rob a liquor store?"

"No." Jo picked at her cuticle. "But we're all sinners, aren't we, Daddy?"

He patted Jo on the back. She knew he'd like that answer. It's what he said just yesterday when her little sister Loralie drew on their bedroom wall. Everyone's a sinner and everyone has to take responsibility for their sins.

Ma had to mix oatmeal into Loralie's bathwater for the welts, after she took responsibility for her sins.

"We didn't all raise junkies, Emmett." Daddy sneered.

Uncle Emmett froze. Leave it to her Daddy to dump a bucket of ice water on any conversation. There was a reason Uncle Emmett's daughter—Jo's cousin Kaitlyn—wasn't allowed in Daddy's house. Jo hadn't seen her since last Christmas when Aunt Clarice caught her stealing from Granny's jewelry box.

Daddy lifted his chin. He hitched his thumb behind his belt buckle and tugged. Everyone's clothes were feeling tight after so much home cooking. "You don't mind your uncle. Go get Daddy a cherry Pepsi."

Jo slid across the back wall to avoid talking to anyone else. Her stomach hurt all of a sudden. Her mouth tasted yeasty like old cereal.

"Hannie?"

She brushed by her Ma and out the screen door. The night was alive with singing cicadas. Down the mountainside, Jo saw the lights in town flickering like the reflection of stars.

"Baby," Ma's hands fluttered around Jo's shoulders like nervous birds, "you're letting all the heat out. Is something wrong?"

Jo swallowed. Her stomach settled as soon as she was away from the crowd. She closed the door. "I'm fine. Sorry, ma'am."

Ma scraped Jo's hair off her forehead. Her sharp nails raked her scalp. Jo leaned into it. "Alright, alright. How about you have a Sprite?"

"No thank you, ma'am. Daddy wants me to get him a drink." She set a hand on the kitchen table. It was wet with steamy condensation.

"Let me pour it." Ma bent to grab the two-liter from the floor beside the fridge. Her shirt rode up. Her back was stained with purple bruises.

"I'll get it!" Jo darted over. She cracked it open and gave the bottle a second to hiss. "Ma?"

"Yes?"

"Were you afraid the first time you took up snakes?"

"No." Ma shook her head. Her ponytail swung. "But I was the first time I drank strychnine."

Jo stuck her tongue out. She cracked the ice tray to release a few cubes. Guests got bagged ice from the corner store, but Daddy only liked ones made with tap water. Jo wasn't looking forward to drinking poison. Daddy said she wouldn't have to for a long time. He said you shouldn't drink strychnine until you could legally drink whiskey.

"I know the Lord protects us so long as we're properly faithful and repent for our sins against him. I know that. Doesn't mean there wasn't something awful about seeing the skull and crossbones on the bottle." Ma shook her head at the memory. She smoothed out the collar of Jo's church blouse. "Were you scared today, baby?"

"No, ma'am." Jo frowned. "Ma, why don't you go outside and have a smoke. You've been working all night keeping everybody fed. You deserve a break."

"Hannie! You know I can't do that."

"Please? I'll get the cornbread out before it burns, if that's what you're worried about."

Ma looked tempted. "I couldn't just leave you here to fend for yourself."

"Why not? If I can take up snakes I can keep a pot of peas from boiling over."

Ma reached down and touched the pack of smokes bulging in her apron pocket. "Five minutes. Not a second more."

Ma grabbed the egg timer on her way out. Jo knew she'd set it and be back before it buzzed.

She didn't have much time.

There weren't any baby locks on the cabinet under the sink. Sarah Lynn was starting to get into everything, but Daddy refused to be inconvenienced in his own home. He liked to keep the drinking-strychnine in the fridge, but run-of-the-mill rat poison was different.

They got infestations every winter. Last year, Daddy got the apple-flavored stuff to make sure the rats ate every last thing. Uncle Emmett ribbed him. Daddy made the congregation drink the nastiest tasting stuff on the market, but the rats ate good.

The label said: *Causes internal bleeding. If ingested, call poison control.*

Jo giggled. Nobody in this house would ever do that.

She poured it in first, then the Pepsi on top. It didn't smell off, although it didn't fizz as much as it should. She mixed it with a plastic spoon until it was nice and combined.

"Johannah?" Daddy called.

"Coming, Daddy!"

When someone repents for their sins, they can drink any deadly thing and it shall not hurt them.

Emily Bay Moore is a writer and archivist living just outside Washington DC. She is in the process of getting her Master's Degree in Library and Information Science at the University of Maryland, College Park. Her research focus is post-mortem privacy policy. Her other works can be found in Lacunae Magazine *and scattered through various Noir at the Bars. She's on twitter @MLE_Bay*

The Legend of Founder's Day

By Copper Smith

Even after Kendall walked into the room and took a seat facing everybody, they just kept talking. Like a class of junior high girls before the teacher got there. Like they didn't see that six-foot-seven Indian step inside and address them.

Kendall didn't care. He just sipped his coffee and waited for everybody to shut up. When they didn't, he said fuck it, and started talking anyway. "I knew a guy who stole a canoe once," his voice deep and loud but not screaming. That was just his voice. "In broad daylight."

A few guys looked at him, but kept on gabbing, not paying attention or anything, more like *who is he talking to?*

The Indian went on. "This was at this sporting goods store in Ottawa. It's not there anymore. I think there's now a place there that sells ceramics. But I'm not sure."

A few guys shut up, sent him their gaze.

"How did he do it? How did he steal a goddamn canoe in broad daylight? With the store open?"

He was getting their attention now.

"He just walked in and took it. Walked over to the place where the boats were, lifted it off the rack, walked out with it."

Quiet enough to hear a mouse pissing on cotton now.

"The salesman, the girl who works the registers, the other girl who works at the other register. The customers. They all figured it must be his. He must have bought it, right? Told them he'd come back, pick it up later after he could get his truck, something like that. Who'd be crazy enough to just walk in and take a canoe?"

Eyes were narrowing now, every face motionless.

The Indian repeated, "Who'd be crazy enough to just walk in a take a canoe?"

"What that got to do with the job we here for?" Dupree asked.

Kendall took another sip. "That's how we're going to do this job. The bank."

"We gon' walk in, take the money, and leave?"

"No. We're gonna be like my friend with the canoe. We're gonna act like everything is just like it's supposed to be. And everybody's going to see us acting that way and think everything is just like it's supposed to be. Here's how we do that: we walk in armed, everybody with a gun. We give a note to the teller, take the money, then leave."

Everybody sat in confused silence, glances exchanged. "How we gonna do that?" Tommy asked.

Another sip. "It's gonna be Founder's Day. I'm a Indian. You guys are cowboys. We have guns because I'm a Indian and you guys are cowboys. Also we have masks."

A few titters from the guys, but that didn't bother Kendall. He just waited for them to think about it.

When things quieted down and he saw all four of their heads nodding, he knew they had thought about it.

Dupree asked, "What if the security guard gets antsy, wants to make sure the guns ain't real?"

Kendall shrugged. "He probably won't."

"But what if he do?"

"You do what needs to be done. You've done this kind of thing before. You can improvise. Long as we can get in with no questions asked, we're fine."

"You know that shit's on security cam, right?" Tweek asked.

"We're wearing masks. Because it's Founder's Day."

Murmuring, more nodded heads. This was what Kendall expected because the shit sounded too good to be true. But they had run out of questions. So he went on. "Get here at ten. No lateness. Do you understand that?"

Reluctant nods.

"I'll give you all your costumes and masks and guns. From then on, you listen to me and only me."

Kendall stood. He probably didn't have to, but this seemed like a good time to remind the guys that he was a big motherfucker and not scared of anybody.

Not Dupree, the tall skinny one with the scar on his nose that everybody knew was from falling off a ladder but it looked badass anyway.

Not Tommy, crazy Irish fuck with a history of punching dudes in the throat if he thought they didn't deserve their girlfriends.

Not Tweek, crack addict who was alright when he got what he needed, but otherwise, watch out because he'd figure out a way to stab you when you weren't looking.

Not Ray Ray, Dupree's son, quiet and barely nineteen,

but he'd just helped plan and pull off a complicated home invasion that ended with him taking out three guys and a Doberman.

"Anybody got any questions?" the Indian asked.

"How much of a take are we looking at?" Tweek asked.

"Should be about eleven thousand. I take the money, I count it, I divide it. We all go home and tell our wives we got the money from, you know, bingo or something. I don't know, make up your own shit. But don't all say 'bingo' because if the wives start asking around they'll be like, 'wait, they couldn't all win that much at bingo.'"

With everything quiet, it was time to take off. Lurlene was at the door, all ninety pounds of her, pointing to her watch to let Kendall know she needed the office back. "Okay, see you all at ten tomorrow."

The guys took their time strolling out of the office, not even pretending not to look at Lurlene's ass as they passed by. Once they were alone, she closed the door and folded her arms. "You gonna tell me what was going on in here?"

* * *

Founder's Day was a local holiday that commemorated the founding of Fort Linwood, Arkansas. According to lore, the occasion was established on the day of the first white man's arrival and the subsequent kinship that took place between them and members of the Choctaw Tribe or some such bullshit, but mostly it was just people dressed up as cowboys and Indians and going to parades and holding sales.

The parade routes clogged the streets on the way to

the bank just like they knew it would. All those cap gun cowboys, towheaded Indians, concession stands selling synthetic headdresses and plastic spears, Mexican cowboys selling Freedom burritos, cowgirls with star spangled lip gloss and red, white, and blue fishnets.

Kendall had talked Lurlene into driving the van, because much as she complained about his "lifestyle," she was kind of intrigued by it and wanted to be involved.

There wasn't much talking on the way there because there wasn't much to talk about. Just guys making sure their masks were on and their guns were properly loaded.

They'd already been through the plan, the little plan there was. Basically, it was keep quiet, take the money, and Lurlene will pull up at the front door in the van. If all went well, they just had to stand there and be prepared for if things stopped going well.

Tommy, Ray Ray, and Dupree sat on one side. Tweek next to Kendall, twirling his gun around a finger until he could see Kendall didn't like it, so he stopped.

"Got damn," Tweek said. "Just like some Clint Eastwood shit. What was my man's name in *High Plains Drifter*? What was his name?"

"He didn't have no name," Dupree answered. "He didn't never have no names. That's my man, Clint Eastwood. No names. He come and go, don't know who the fuck he is."

"Harry Callahan was a name," Tommy said, not looking up from his gun.

"What?" Dupree asked.

"That was his name in the Dirty Harry movies. Harry Callahan. You said he never has a name."

"That shit don't count," Dupree said. "I'm talking about westerns. You see that motherfucker in a western, he ain't got shit to say and ain't got no name. And if he do have a name, don't nobody know it. That's my man."

Ray Ray leaned back, eyes busy like he was studying everybody.

Dupree pulled his revolver out, tapped open the chamber, sent the bullets to his lap. "Check it out," he said to his son.

Ray Ray sent his eyes to the weapon, but otherwise didn't move.

"This shit here's a single-action. Old school. That means you can't just fire and keep firing like you can with a double-action or a pistol. You got to pull that hammer back each time." He demonstrated.

The Indian watched their faces, going back and forth. The way they talked, the way their words wove together. It was kind of like music. He wondered if this was a thing with all fathers and sons or just Dupree and Ray Ray.

"Wait, we all have single-action revolvers?" Tommy asked the Indian. "Why'd you get that kind?"

"Realistic," Kendall said. "Cowboys had single-action revolvers, so that's what you have."

Tweek started twirling the gun again. "Cowboys was some bad motherfuckers. Boys had some heart. Out in the old west, sun beating down, Indians on they asses. That took some heart."

"No," Kendall said.

"No?" Tweek asked. "What was wrong with them?"

"They were not brave. Not strong."

"Uh-huh, you done started some shit," Dupree chuckled, hands raised in surrender. "You fucking with his peeps now. I'm gon' step back from that one." Laughter all around, even Ray Ray cracked the first smile anybody had seen.

But not Kendall. "Let's focus on the job. No more joking."

* * *

The Indian walked in first, followed by the cowboys. They brought smiles to every face—assuring smiles. They nodded with familiarity, like somebody stepping into a comfortable pair of slippers. Nothing new, nothing unusual. Just another Founder's Day. So far, so good.

They got in line, more smiles and nods. The only gawker was a ten-year-old firing finger gun shots at the Indian as his mama gave his hand a yank. "Will you come on before we miss the parade!" she urged.

The line of seven people soon became five. Kendall let Dupree step in front of him, then Tommy and Tweek. The plan demanded he be in the rear to keep an eye on things. But a grin from the security guard in back suggested he'd soon regret that.

The guard could have been nineteen or thirty, hard to tell. He smiled with too many teeth and laughed at everything. Curly blonde hair, freckles. He leaned in, eyed Kendall, then pulled back and aimed a shout behind the teller's counter. "This one's looking pretty real, Wade!"

The Indian said nothing and did nothing but watched everything, hands clasped at his waist.

He saw Wade glance up from behind the counter, balding, men's dress shirt and vest like he wanted to remind people he was important. He said, "He might be real. You ask him?"

The guard turned. "You a real Indian?"

Kendall shook his head. Saying yes would mean the

police would be looking for an actual Indian.

"I didn't think so. Those ain't even authentic feathers."

Kendall smiled, but only on the inside. He had thought of everything. Even the fake headdress when he could have easily gotten his hands on a real one.

Everybody moved up in line, but the guard wasn't done with him yet. "The gun looks real though."

Kendall nodded.

"Let me see it."

Tweek panicked, turned to them, eyes alert.

Kendall said, "Sorry, can't do that. They don't let me. These replicas are expensive."

"Aw, come on! You can bend the rules this once."

"Maybe next year." Everybody moved up in line again.

"Tell you what," the guard said, tugging his gun from the holster and offering it butt first. "You can hold my real one while I hold yours."

Dupree looked back. Tommy too. Everybody moved up in line.

The Indian eyed the guard's gun. A Sig Sauer P365, which held a ten-round flush fit magazine. Not like his single-action revolver with five rounds. He reached into his holster, pulled out the revolver, and made the exchange.

The security guard weighed the revolver in his hand, mouth puckered, eyebrows up. "Good night, Gladys! Does this thing ever look as real as real can look!" He twirled it over his head, calling to behind the counter again. "Hey, Wade! Check me out! I'm a cowboy eeeeee-hawwwww!"

The guard looked behind the counter, waiting for a reaction.

But Wade's attention seemed pulled away. Dupree had reached the front of the line and slid the note across the counter.

Wade stood next to the teller, a lady with stacked auburn hair and too much lipstick. Her eyes got big after reading the note, but Wade just nodded slowly to Dupree.

"Wade?" The guard called.

The lady handed over a thick envelope. Wade kept nodding.

"Wade!" The guard called again, impatient now. "Check out how authentic this thing is!"

Kendall was watching Dupree so closely as he took the money and tucked it away, he barely noticed the hammer of his revolver getting pulled back.

He turned to the guard too late.

"Hands up, Tonto!" The guard giggled, barrel at the Indian's temple, finger on the trigger. "Watch this, Wade!" In a bad John Wayne, he said, "I'm gonna shoot me a redskin!"

Kendall tried to reach into his holster and fish out the guard's Sig Sauer, but he couldn't get there before the shot clapped out. Luckily, it was Dupree's shot.

It stung at everybody's ears, loud, sharp, angry. With it came jolted bodies, screams, hands covering faces.

All eyes went to the guard's quaking body, slamming against the wall, geyser of blood painting his chest, legs flailing, torso buckling, curled fingers clawing at his neck as he pushed out choppy sandpaper breaths on his way to the carpet.

An alarm rang—a long, deep wail—but the screams smothered it to a whimper.

Kendall turned to the counter, found Dupree holding

his pose, admiring his bullseye like a painter leaning back from the canvas. He also spotted Wade ducking behind the counter, then popping up seconds later, rifle in hand. "Look out!" he shouted, then ducked behind a desk.

Voices threaded into one long screech, eyes now aimed everywhere, bedlam, scrambling bodies crashing in the chaos, racing for the door.

Kendall and Dupree fired three shots in Wade's direction, but he had ducked again, then risen to the window two tellers down and taken another shot.

"Shit!" Tommy called, taking one to the chest, knees pounding the floor as he fired again, but missed.

Wade shot again and clipped Tommy's shoulder, sending him down for good.

Dupree and Tweek found shelter behind a wooden stand, but Ray Ray found nothing. Wade nicked him on the knee as he sprinted for the stand, bringing him to the carpet, all groans and useless flopping.

His dad reached out and dragged his drained body behind the stand as two more shots from Wade missed.

The frenzied screamers had raced free, leaving the center clear of obstacles and the lobby eerily quiet. A short calm interrupted, the only sounds were mumbled prayers behind the counter and the alarm's nagging drone.

Positions were fixed now: Kendall behind the desk, the guard's Sig Sauer in one hand, plus he'd scooped up his own revolver.

Dupree, Tweek, and Ray Ray behind the stand, guns out, but nothing from the younger man but more groans, knees pulled to his chest as his face became all teeth and widened eyes.

Behind the teller's counter, it was Whac-A-Mole now, with Wade firing from a window, then ducking down and popping up, firing from a different window, face fixed in a crazed grimace.

The Indian surveyed things, saw the other three closer to the door, Lurlene safely outside in the van as Dupree clutched the envelope. He could see them whisper between them, planning a trip out.

Tweek rose up, tried to get to Wade, but his timing was bad and he caught one that snapped his head back, putting a crimson fountain where his jaw used to be. He tried to hold himself up on the stand, but that only slowed his body's drop to the carpet, limp and lifeless before he got there.

When Wade came up again, firing a few more times, Kendall followed, shot back. The guys behind the stand made a break for the door.

Wade ducked down again, popped up at a window closer to the door, taking aim at the escapees. He clipped the kid again, getting him in the ankle.

Kendall shot back, sent Wade ducking for cover as Ray Ray's groans washed everything out. The alarm, the screams, the sirens in the distance. It echoed through the bank like a bad trumpet player punishing his upstairs neighbors.

Ray Ray stretched his arms out, his dad reaching back for him, eyes gigantic as his head swiveled from the counter to his kid, then back again.

Wade popped up, rifle aimed at Ray Ray, so Kendall had no choice. He stood, guns out, charged the counter, firing away. This brought the rifleman's scope to a new target, giving Dupree the time he needed to pull his son to freedom, dragging him to the van outside.

Everything ended in a blur for the Indian, too much pain until he felt nothing, black filled his vision as he tumbled away from it all.

* * *

Years later, people still talk about the Founder's Day shooting. They talk about the day a crazed Indian stormed into the bank and took hostages along with some helpers who got away. According to lore, the Indian didn't get away. He tried to attack the bank manager—Wade Macalister (later the town's mayor). The Indian, it seemed, needed one more scalp to be recognized as tribal leader. But Wade was determined not to let him get that scalp, so he charged the Indian, rifle blazing, and shot him down against all odds.

Ray Ray tells the story a little differently.

Copper Smith creates fictional mayhem in Minneapolis, mostly in the form of gritty post-apocalyptic noir. He enjoys playing guitar in bands that deserve better and describing himself in the third person. He does a twitter thing. @CopperNoir.

Good Old Days

By Rob Pierce

"Hey, Reno."

It was Casey. "Yeah?"

"You hear?"

"I hear what?"

"You don't pay no attention to the news?"

"What the fuck happened, Casey?"

"They dredged up the car."

I lit a cigarette, sat up in bed. It wasn't early, just for me. "What car?"

"The Lincoln Town Car."

"Meet me at Benny's. An hour?"

"Yeah, sure."

Benny's was a beer and breakfast joint, breakfast all day, twenty-four hours. They catered to an interesting crowd. Bunch of guys you might see in the joint, if you were unlucky.

I ordered coffee, bacon and eggs, waited for Casey. The waitress didn't have a name tag for some reason.

"What's your name, honey?"

"Shelly." She said it blank faced, like I was hitting on

41

her. Believe me, I wasn't. She was pretty, blonde, and thin, the last thing I wanted.

I nodded and she walked away.

The job with the Town Car went back a bunch of years. My plate was almost empty when Casey walked in and sat across from me. We were at a table, far from the counter. The counter was for guys with less private things to discuss.

"So," I said, "the Lincoln."

"Yeah."

"They find any blood?"

"It's more than a decade, it washed away. Along with the upholstery."

"And they didn't find the body."

Shelly came by, refilled my coffee and poured one for Casey, asked if there'd be anything else. Casey shook his head.

"Maybe later," I said. "I'll letcha know."

Didn't want her dropping by mid-story.

"The body," I said.

"Fuck no. We dumped that a mile away. Fish food by now."

"The good old days." We both laughed.

But the day we dumped that car in the river was especially good. We stole it that morning, robbed the bank that afternoon, and an hour after the robbery, pulled up to the riverbank. We left the car in drive and pushed. Me and Casey pushed; not such a good afternoon for Harvey. He was part of our crew and it was his blood on the backseat, a lot of it. The bastards shot him. He bled fast, faster than we could get him to any docs we knew.

Harder work than it would have been with him,

pushing the car in. But it did increase our shares from a third each to a half, so we were happy about that part. I mean, he was gone, that was just bad luck, could have been either of us. So when we went out later, we started by raising a glass to lost friends. A couple of others in the bar heard our toast and raised their glasses. A lotta guys out there with friends shot to death.

Truth, though, Harvey was more a partner than a friend, same as Casey, but ideally he'd have been there with us and we'd have skipped the toast. We'd fit all the money into my travel bag, which sat on the floor beneath me, my feet resting on it. After a few rounds we got a cab back to the crash pad and split the money, then two more cabs to our separate apartments. That all went smooth, including getting back sober enough for an even split.

It was a hefty chunk of cash and took a while to count, a reasonable trade-off. We made it back to our places, lived on that money a while. No one looks for marked bills when you're in a restaurant in another state. Or a whorehouse.

"So," I said to Casey, "you ain't worried, are ya? You saw the news. How long ago they say the job was?"

"They didn't talk about the job. They just said the car was stolen fourteen years ago."

"And we pulled the job the same day."

"Yeah."

I'd finished my breakfast and when we finished our coffees, I flagged down Shelly. She brought the coffee and started to refill but I shook my head and she stopped.

"What kinda beers you got, Shell?"

She recited the list and we each ordered one.

"So," I said when she'd stepped away, "you antsy?"

"I guess."

"About what?"

"I dunno."

Shelly brought our beers.

"Thanks, hon," I said, and she skirted away.

"Man, you got her on edge."

"Kids these days. So fucking sensitive."

He nodded. He agreed with me, but he was getting sensitive too.

"What the fuck is it, Casey?"

"It's about the car."

"What's about the car?"

"We should go back, make sure it's clean."

"Jesus Christ." I drank. "How long a fucking bath it gotta take? You wanna see it wrinkled?"

"Nah, man. It's just..."

I swear, every word felt designed to piss me off. "Just what?"

"Just..." and he whispered the rest, too soft for me to hear.

"Okay. We ain't gonna talk. We got the beers, let's drink. You gotta whisper, we go somewhere and talk."

Asshole had me worried. Like I said, we weren't friends. We drank and paid. I said good night to Shelley. I was amused, she wasn't. Like I said, fucking kids.

Anyway, in the parking lot he could talk above a whisper.

"That car," he said. "Harvey died there. Our accomplice in a armed robbery. That makes us, murder one."

"Fuck, Casey. It's a long time."

"Ain't no statue of whaddayacallits on murder, Reno."

"Okay. Chill. Lemme think through this. I'll figure

the best way to deal with it."

The best way would be if I had a piece on me, I'd take this stupid shit into the woods and blow his head off. But I wasn't packing, I was out for breakfast with a former partner. A guy who'd lost all his nerve. Only one way for this to end.

"Give it a day," I said. "I call ya tomorrow."

After I grab a pistol and figure how to get rid of the body, asshole. Never shoulda split that money with him. Coulda raised that toast alone, him dead in the river too. Woulda been harder to push the car in that way, but I'd have managed. Just needed fourteen years notice that Casey was gonna lose it.

Home, I grabbed a .38, checked the cartridge, one in the chamber too. Put it in tomorrow's jacket, hung it over a chair. I grabbed a fifth, half full, didn't bother with a glass. I wouldn't sleep tonight. Casey used to be a good guy. I drank, drank some more. I got so drunk I proved myself wrong. I passed out.

* * *

I woke up. I didn't look forward to it. My head throbbed. Aspirin on the bedside table, I popped a few. Looked at my watch. Just past noon. Shit, I wanted to sleep in. I sat up in bed, kicked aside the empty bottle that lay on its side on the floor. I needed coffee. God, I needed coffee.

I staggered to the kitchen, grateful for the furniture I could cling to on the way, the walls I leaned on. Regret in advance, I guess. Casey should not have gone crazy, should have got to stay alive. I didn't know if it was choices. Brains sometimes go. I'd seen it in my mom, dementia, but she was old by the time she started mixing me up with Dad. Thank God she didn't like him, I'd had no desire to tell Mom I couldn't fuck her. Like I had no desire to kill this stupid piece of shit. Damn you, Casey.

I braced myself against the counter as I made the coffee. Felt like I should be able to just chew on the granules. Maybe if they were beans, but then I'd have to have a grinder and keep it clean and fuck that, this was bad enough. Didn't have to deal with the sound of grinding beans, just waited for the water to boil, then poured.

I put on more water as soon as I'd poured a cup, knew I'd need two. I'd put this off another day but that wouldn't help, I'd get twice as drunk tonight.

I drank the coffee, then the second cup, took a shower, threw on a shirt and jeans and boots, grabbed the jacket from the chair and walked out the door. Called Casey from the hall, set up a meet. Decided against the woods. Along the riverbank would do. Would do justice.

I stood there, chewing on a cigarette, lit it when I heard him approach.

"Case."

"Hey, Reno. We going?"

"To the car? I don't know, man. That still what you want to do?"

"We got to, man."

"That's how they involve us. Cops have that car now. We gotta go where they stash evidence. Their yard. Cops guard that."

He nodded. "So, you was up all night figuring how to get past the guard?"

"Ain't like that, Case."

"You tell me, Reno. What's it like?"

I couldn't answer, not in words. I looked down, frowned, put a hand in my coat pocket and looked up, held it on him.

"Shit, Reno, no."

"You're gonna crack, Case. You crack, we both die."

I shot him in the gut. I knew a gut shot hurt like hell and wouldn't kill him right away, but I couldn't bring myself to shoot him in the head.

"Fuck, Reno. Fuck."

"Sorry it came to this, Case. Only way."

"I hoped the only way would be us going to the car."

"That was impossible, Case."

He was grimacing. I was tempted to shoot him in the head and put him out of his misery.

"I already talked, Reno. Whatcha call a cooperative witness." Took him forever to say that much.

"Talked? To who?"

"FBI," he said, his eyes closing.

I heard people running toward us. "Shit."

I shot Casey in the head, raised the .38 to my temple, and fired.

Rob Pierce wrote the novels Blood By Choice, Tommy Shakes, Uncle Dust, *and* With the Right Enemies, *the novella* Vern in the Heat, *and the short story collection* The Things I Love Will Kill Me Yet. *All books are available at AllDueRespect.com, as well as via the usual slumlords. He lives and will probably die in Oakland, California.*

Squid Lord

By K. A. Laity

It was him, all right. Somehow he had known it all along. He could blame it on that bloody corner shop. That's where she met him—the celebrity chef. Or what passed for a 'celebrity' in this squalid little seaside town. Calamari King, my arse.

Squid Lord: that was more like it.

The first day she had run into him there, buying the daily wotsits. She always had some reason to go— mostly to see what was going on, get the local gossip, buy the lottery tickets Dan told her not to waste her money on—but that day had been memorable, mostly for how much she irritated him going on about it. Dan liked to think of himself as a tolerant man, but Harley really got up his nose that day.

'Only guess who I met. He only lives round the corner. Can you believe it? And him such a success. Our neighbourhood. And he says he might have a job for me.' He hated the way her face glowed with excitement over him. Not like she'd had that glow for himself for some time. Nothing but nags for him. Not his fault he'd been out of work these past few months. That manager had it coming, the whiny little streak of piss.

'What job?' he had finally muttered after she went on and on about his stylish look, those grey turnup trousers and his mane of white hair. Mane! She actually called it that like he was a lion or something. Just another sheep shagger in this broken-down ex-mill town, even if he did have aspirations to make a name for himself. Good luck with that. Local celebrity don't travel down the road much.

'A hostess!' Harley giggled and he should have guessed it then.

'What's that? Serving cake and coffee?' He snorted.

'No, silly. Greeting people at the door, walking them to their tables when it's not busy or handing the menus to the waitstaff if you are. I'd be the face of the restaurant.' She preened, actually preened. Harley did have a nice face but right then he wanted nothing more than to push a grapefruit into it and make her pucker up.

'Face of the restaurant? And what about the arse?'

'Fuck you, it's work.' Harley lost her grin. 'One of us has got to and it looks like you've given up on that front.'

Naturally enough that resulted in another barney that went on and on until it was too late, and he was on the couch yet again because the world made him mad and there was nobody but her to take it out on. He couldn't afford to go out on the lash with the lads anymore and complain with them.

So he laid off on the matter, hoping to get back into Harley's good graces and into the marital bed. She wasn't a woman who could do without for long, so he had hopes that her cold mood would thaw. He needed that second chance to prove he could be supportive.

Dan complimented her on that first night as hostess. She did look smashing. He thought she'd wear a uniform like when she was working at Peg Leg Reg's café, but Harley dressed like she was going out with those mad gals she'd known since forever who scared him a bit, who careered through the town like a permanent hen party every fortnight or so, their faces made up like fashion dolls.

'You look fab, Harl.' Dan gave her a peck on the cheek, hoping the peace offering would be accepted. She was nervous enough to take little notice of it, checking her brows in the little mirror she kept in her handbag and rooting around for the just right shade of lipstick for the downplayed lighting.

'I'm so nervous. The face of the restaurant! It's a huge responsibility.' She looked solemn as a nun taking vows—oh, the irony.

'You'll do great,' Dan had reassured her, giving her a little smack on the bottom as she headed out to catch the bus.

And here he was six weeks later hoping to surprise her at the end of the shift and instead staring through the window of the Squid Lord's office as he watched the celebrity chef knead his wife's arse like it was bread. Their tongues were wrapped together like tentacles. Harley was pulling her skirt up. The chef pressed her down on the desktop and then reached up to tear down her knickers. Dan could feel his face hot with fury but damn if there wasn't something arousing about it too, which only made him more furious.

The damn Squid Lord getting what he wasn't? And making a meal of it, too: damn, but Harley had nice tits. He could almost taste them. But that fucking chef!

Literally, in this case. Look at them! Christ, that couldn't be comfortable, could it?

At last Dan tore himself away—fuming, horny and resentful. He thought of confronting her when she got home that night, but she looked so damn happy that he was confused and sort of ashamed. Why hadn't she been that happy for him? Harley pecked him on the cheek and jumped in the shower, saying she had to get the food smell off her. Squid, no doubt. It was the signature dish after all. He wanted to ask her how the squid tasted tonight, but the rage rendered him mute.

Dan lay awake beside her—at least she had warmed up enough to allow him back in the bed—angry, aroused, resentful. He thought of trying to get her interested but her snores suggested he had missed the window of opportunity. At last he got up and went to the bathroom and took care of himself as he had done for many months now.

He couldn't stop picturing her with the Squid Lord.

Dan sat on the edge of the tub after washing up. He wanted to kill the man—with his mane of white hair and all. Squid Lord: would he bleed ink? He'd have to make it look like an accident, so he wouldn't end up in the clink himself. Harley would be sorry then. She'd want him back. They'd have a second chance.

But how to do it?

It was late. He didn't have a lot of ideas. Maybe he needed to sleep on it. In the morning he might feel different anyway. The feelings you had at a sleepless three a.m. didn't always last in the harsh light of the morning. A grey day though, and he might well think hard on it.

Dan woke up late, feeling hungover though he'd not even had so much as a pint the night before. Harley was away. She often went 'shopping' during the day. Now he wondered if she was really at the stores or if she was shagging the Squid Lord somewhere. His anger was pure and cold now. He'd seen enough crime shows to know he had to be careful, but revenge was necessary now. It would make him feel whole again. Harley would respond to that, he was sure.

Dan prepared to be all shifty and quiet like a detective. The truth was most people didn't give a toss about the world around them and that went double for the Squid Lord. It was a doddle finding his house among the trim buildings on the other side of the dual carriageway. They were a nicer set than the lot they lived in, though not as much nicer as he would have expected for a celebrity like him. Maybe he was salting his money away to keep a whole string of dollies. If he was cheating with Harley, chances were he was cheating with others.

That was how Dan spotted the wife. Of course the Squid Lord was married. His wife didn't seem to work. She was always about the house with one of those little rat dogs scampering around her feet. He could just peek into their back garden from the bus shelter across the way. Well, he had to stand on the bench to get that peek. Dan didn't think it drew too much attention though; people seemed to expect daft behaviour in this town.

He was trying to think of some excuse for ringing her doorbell so he could size her up when she popped out to walk the little yapper. Dan casually strolled along like he had nowhere better to be. The wife looked nice in that reality star kind of way, which is to say too much makeup and bizarre-coloured clothes that were probably something fashionable. The little dog had a diamante collar and lead. They made the picture of prosperity.

Dan rehearsed some conversational starters in case the opportunity arose to start something with her. He'd pump her for information like those detectives do if she ever got off her mobile. God, he'd hate to have been on the other end of that conversation. He couldn't quite hear her, but there was no mistaking the body language of a woman who was angry.

Then he got a break. Well, the dog made a break for it, lunging away from her toward some bright wrapper that wafted by on the pavement. Dan pelted after it and grabbed the lead just before the little bugger would have run into traffic and ended up a pancake under a cab's wheels.

'Hey there, little guy, er gal,' Dan said, reeling the wiggly little creature in. The fat pug was wheezing with the small effort it had made. Horrible little thing but at least it didn't try to bite. He turned to the dog's mistress to see her scowling. 'Caught the little darling just in time.'

'Thanks,' she said without any warmth, taking the dog from him. Her face had the pinched look of someone in a permanent bad mood. Maybe her husband was the reason. 'Honestly it might be better for all if she had been squashed.'

'Oh, it can't be as bad as that, can it?' Dan said with as much sympathy as he could muster.

'It's worse than that,' she muttered, a dark look across her brow. Her nails were lacquered blood red, as if she were ready to rip someone's heart out.

'Fancy a cuppa? You look like you could use a good sit down and a chat.' He wanted the chance to pump her for information, why not let her think he was attracted.

With that dog snorting in her arms it was more of a challenge, but he saw her face move a little away from stormy weather toward the sunny side of the street.

'You one of those swinger dudes?' She arched one eyebrow at him and gave him the once over. Dan always wondered how women did that. He could only ever raise both eyebrows and look surprised. That one eyebrow trick made any statement sound dubious.

'Oh, you think I'm trying to pick you up? I suppose beautiful women have to face that a lot.' When in doubt, flatter flatter flatter. It was a rule Dan stuck to with some success over the years.

She gave a short bark of laughter then stuck out blood-red tipped claws. 'I'm BZ.'

Dan took her hand and wondered if he'd misheard. 'BZ or you saying you're busy? I'm Dan in any case.' Belatedly he wondered if he ought to have given a false name. This criminal business didn't come natural to him.

'It's a nickname. Since childhood. Even I don't remember where it came from.' Now that was a smile—a genuine one. She looked miles better with it on, even with the snorting dog. 'Oh, why not. Shall we go to Smith's?'

They sat in the dingy little café Dan came to know most of her life. It came pouring out of her like a fallen film star to talking to the gutter press. She covered the lot—all about her life in the Midlands and how she hated the north and this town and most of all that she wouldn't mind someone killing the Squid Lord, who was called Benjy, daft name for an adult.

At least that was Dan's impression of the situation and he approved of her malice. He also fancied there was a good chance of getting a leg over after she invited him back to the house, so he kept up a stream of compliments and sympathetic sounds. BZ broke out the wine and he knew he was in like Flynn. They adjourned to the bedroom—*her* bedroom, it turned out. That's how far south things had gone with them. Dan marveled at the luxury of it. This chef must be loaded.

It wasn't his best effort, to be truthful. For one thing BZ wasn't all that exciting. She looked well enough a goer but in bed she wasn't a patch on Harley, who was even better when she was angry. A little enthusiasm would have helped a lot. Dan had to admit that ol' Benjy definitely took a step up with his wife. Nevertheless, if it helped seal the deal, it was worth the effort. And having a real woman instead of his own hand was a welcome change even if she did make him wrap it up. 'Safety first,' she had slurred at him, opening the nightstand drawer to show off a wide variety of condoms in rainbow colours and a few sexual aids as the magazines called them.

The thought did cross his mind to wonder if he ought to be using them with Harley once he got back in her good graces. Can't be too careful. Working with squid probably wasn't all that hygienic and he had seen no sign of protection when they were doing it on the desk that night. Sadly, remembering his window-cleaner lookeeloo had put him over the edge at last when the unhelpful BZ just kind of lay there. He'd never had to resort to fantasizing when he was actually with a woman.

It was a sad state of things he had come to. Murder was the only way back.

In the end it wasn't difficult to convince her. When he casually suggested that life would be better without the Squid Lord around, BZ said, 'We could make it look like an accident.' Apparently she was an even bigger fan of crime tales. She had it all worked out, see? Just waiting to find a willing accomplice. It turned out she knew all about Harley—and where the chef parked his squid these days.

BZ still took care of the banking for the restaurant so Benjy couldn't hide any cash from her. She also kept the insurance full on and up to date. Not only was the Squid Lord swimming in it—everything he had was fully insured. So all they needed was one of his late night rendezvous, a cosh to the head, the gas 'leaking' and a fire lit. Boom, problem over, riches to share. As long as the blow to his noggin didn't break anything, there was no way the forensics could sniff out a deliberate act. In tedious detail, BZ regaled him with the plot of some novel that hinged on just such a scheme. He would Google it later just to be sure: totally legit.

There might not be enough of him left to forensic anyway.

They picked Friday night. Harley had a habit of working really late on Fridays so he deducted that was their 'special' night. Of course he had to do the GBH himself. BZ, as the primary beneficiary as the insurance forms termed it, had to be above suspicion and elsewhere with an air-tight alibi for the whole thing to work.

Dan had a bad night or two thinking about the plan—half nervous to just get to it and a little guilty at ending a life. Then he stared at her back and thought about how the Squid Lord had robbed him of his wife's attention and favours. Her face turned away from him every night now. And it wasn't like he was killing him. He was only knocking him on the head. The rest was science. It wasn't his fault if the Squid Lord was blown up by a chemical reaction.

The night of the crime arrived. Harley went off to work as usual with a smile on her face, while Dan sat flipping channels aimlessly, watching the clock. Would she drop a few tears for the Squid Lord? Miss his tentacles? Probably just a distraction for her, a momentary crush. She was always going on about his intelligence and what was it? His 'business acumen'—what a laugh. She couldn't even explain what that was to Dan, just got all snarky, then blamed him for being dim.

We'll see who has more business acumen, Dan thought with satisfaction as he put on his all-black crime clothes. To avoid any kind of witnesses, he had decided to walk down to the pier. It wasn't that bad of a distance and the night was relatively balmy for early spring. And the city sloped toward the water's edge so it was a doddle. He'd catch a cab on the way back maybe, over by the central station.

The walk did him good. He was feeling rather chipper by the time he got to the restaurant. Even the sight of his wife riding the Squid Lord couldn't dampen his mood too much. *Just you wait, mate—we'll see who gets screwed now.* When Harley came out the back door and clacked away on her heels, Dan came out from behind the bins and slipped in the back door. BZ had been right: he didn't lock up behind her as he planned to be exiting soon himself.

He just didn't know *how* he'd be leaving this time.

Dan took the heavy Mag Lite torch out of the inside pocket of his donkey jacket, ready for action. He could hear the Squid Lord humming away, happy as a clam. He wouldn't be humming for long. Peeking around the end of the corridor, he could see the chef shoving some papers into a filing cabinet. As he rolled the drawer shut, Dan ran into the room and thumped him on the melon and down he went. Just like clockwork.

It wasn't so easy to drag him back out to the kitchen, though. For one thing, he was solid as bricks. The Squid Lord was a lot taller than he remembered, too. Dan lamented giving up the weekend football league a few years ago. He'd been in better shape back then. So far from fit now that he had to stop twice while dragging the man across the tiles. A sad state to be in for sure, but it was better than being dead, he had to admit. He could buy a home gym to get back in shape soon.

Dan propped the chef up against the industrial-size refrigerator and turned his attention to the stove. Criminy, it had a lot of knobs and whatnot. It took a minute to sort out how to work things. He lit one burner and started turning the knobs of the others to get them pouring out the gas into the room. Then he screamed.

A hand gripped his ankle. Dan shook it off and wheeled around.

'Wasssgoinon?' The Squid Lord sounded drunk. He had fallen on his side and was groping about as if he had become blind from the blow. Dan considered whether to hit him again or if that might mess up the forensics if he did it too hard. The chef shook his head like he was just waking up and then lunged at Dan, who backed away quickly. Too quickly—he bumped into the stove. And then he could smell hair burning.

His jacket was on fire!

Dan shuffled the jacket off, dropping his keys, wallet and a handful of change on the tile floor. He tried to shake the fire off, and when that didn't work, threw it to the ground and stomped on it until the smoldering stopped. The dazed chef was trying to get to his feet, so Dan took a chance and cracked his skull again, hoping it wasn't actually literally so. The man crumpled to the tiles again, hopefully this time to stay.

His hands were shaking as Dan gathered up his belongings—fuck the change, he wouldn't need it—stuffed them back in his jacket and headed for the door. He had no idea how long it would take until the place exploded, so he wanted to be sure to be watching it from outside.

His heart was hammering like an alarm bell when he got to the back door. He grabbed the knob and twisted it, then collided with the door. He stared at the handle, twisted it more carefully, then with growing panic turned it this way and that. His heart was in his mouth as he slammed his whole body against the door. Then he stopped.

Out the tiny grimy window he saw Harley and BZ. His own wife held up a key and it twinkled in the moonlight as she swung it back and forth on a chain. The two women had their arms around each other's shoulders. BZ clutched that little rat dog under one arm. They were both grinning like this was the funniest joke ever.

Dan screamed every rotten word he knew at them as they turned and walked away. Then he stopped. Maybe there was still time to turn off the gas—

K. A. Laity is an award-winning author, scholar, critic, editor, and arcane artist. Her books include Chastity Flame, Lush Situation, A Cut-Throat Business, Love is a Grift, The Mangrove Legacy, Satan's Sorority, White Rabbit, *and many more. She has edited* Respectable

Horror, Weird Noir, Noir Carnival, Drag Noir, *and* My Wandering Uterus, *plus written many short stories, scholarly essays, songs, and more.*

Wherever He's Going

By Daniel Vlasaty

"Yo, Dildo, what the fuck?" Frankie says and swats his arm out.

"Wh—huh? What?" Dildo says. He sits up in his seat, wipes at the drool hanging in the corner of his mouth, rubs at his eyes.

Frankie looks at him.

"What?" Dildo says again.

"What do you mean *what?* I said: *what the fuck?*"

Dildo sits up even more in his seat, pinching at the bridge of his nose. "Wh—"

"Don't fucking say *what* again, man. Don't you fucking say it."

"I don—"

"You were talking about whatever the fuck you were talking about and then you stopped talking. Fucking fell asleep over there. Right in the middle of whatever."

"I did? How long was I—"

"How long were you, what? Asleep?" Frankie says. He shrugs his big body, which is something in his tiny ass Honda. "Like ten fucking seconds, man. You were

63

talking about whatever and then"—he snaps his fingers—
"like I fucking said, you were just asleep. Like it's that
thing. You know that one thing, right?" He's snapping his
fingers more now, like that's going to help him remember
shit. "Oh fuck, what's it called?"

Dildo shakes his head. Because Dildo don't know
what the fuck Frankie's talking about.

"You know—" Frankie's still saying, still going on
with whatever this is. "That one fucking thing."

But Dildo barely even knows where he is right now.

Frankie snaps again. "The fucking thing where you
could like fall asleep at any second. You know like you
could be right in the middle of eating dinner, or driving
your car, or shit, I don't know, like right in the middle
of fucking your girl. In the middle of whatever you're
doing and then BAM, you pass the fuck out. Kind of
like you just were."

Dildo's looking around, barely listening to whatever
Frankie's talking about. Trying to piece shit back together
in his brain. Everything's cloudy and he can't remember
where they are or what they're going to do.

He closes his eyes, squeezes them as tight as he can.
Thinking maybe, hopefully, if he squeezes them tight
enough his brain might start working again.

Frankie reaches out and snaps, this time right in
Dildo's face. "You know the fucking thing I'm talking
about, right?"

"Wh—" Dildo starts to say, but stops and waves
Frankie's hand away, says, "Fuck, yeah, dude. I think I
fucking know what you're talking about. Just...I don't
know what it's...Just hold...My head's all—"

But Frankie ignores him, fucking with him now. He
snaps again. Not too close to Dildo this time, but still

close enough that it's obvious he's trying to be a dick about it. "You know what I'm fucking talking about. I know you do. So, what's it called, though?"

"Fuck, I don't know—"

"Come on, Dildo, you fucking know."

And again, with the snapping. All around in Dildo's space.

"Why are you coming at me like—" Dildo says. "Why don't you know what it's called? Why is it—"

"I'm trying to think here, too, man. But I know you know."

He snaps, barely touches the tip of Dildo's nose. "What's it called?" he says. "Come on, motherfucker, I know you know."

Snap.

"Fuck!" Dildo says. He takes a wild haymaker swing at Frankie—not an easy thing in Frankie's stupid and tiny car. Frankie easily blocks it and he's smiling now.

Dildo comes at him again, another wild, terrible punch. "It's called necrophilia or something," he says. "You asshole."

And Frankie stops. He's looking at Dildo and Dildo's breathing all hard. Throwing those two punches took it out of him. He's a mess—sweating and shaking, can't catch his breath.

"Narcolepsy," Frankie says. And he's starting to laugh a bit now.

"What?"

"Narcolepsy," he says again. Laughing harder. "You said it's called necrophilia, but that's where you like jerk off over dead chicks or whatever." He punches his fist against the steering wheel, the whole car shudders. "What I'm talking about, where you just fall asleep like

65

that"—and he snaps again—"that's called narcolepsy."

And now Frankie's rolling with it. He's full-on laughing, busting up. Way down from deep in his gut. His whole body shaking with it.

"Necrophilia," he says, slowing down, kind of chuckling now. "You sick motherfucker, what the fuck—"

And Dildo comes at him again with another swing. This one open-handed. He's swats against Frankie's shoulder without doing much else.

Frankie's laughing again. "What would your mother think? You sick, sad boy."

Dildo swings again. "You asshole. Fuck you. You had me all fucked up with your snapping and my head's all...I...I don't fucking—"

Frankie holds his hands up, he snaps again and says: "Hold up." He points out through the windshield. "There he is."

"There who is?"

"There—who the fuck do you think it is?" Frankie says. "What do you think we're doing here, my man? You fucking—"

Dildo looks around again and he remembers.

"Fuck you," he says as Frankie shifts around in his seat, reaches over, starts the car.

They're quiet as they follow the Escalade through Rogers Park, heading north. Frankie's keeping them back a bit and it's easy enough to follow a giant shining black SUV through the early afternoon traffic, all the tiny hybrid fucking whatever cars that are taking over the neighborhood.

Frankie turns to Dildo. "You're acting all fucked up

here and I need to make sure you're going to be okay to do this thing with me."

Dildo's rubbing at his eyes again, shifting in his seat. Frankie's not an idiot. Frankie can see what this is, what's going on with Dildo.

"Yeah," Dildo says. "Yeah, whatever. Can't we do it like right here?"

"What? You got somewhere else you need to be right now, got something else you'd rather be doing?"

Fucking with him, really going with it.

"I'm just saying," Dildo says. "We're here right now, we could get it done now and then that's it, we're done. Don't got to be doing this following around thing all fucking day."

Frankie shakes his head.

"What?"

"Fuck you, *what*. You fucking asshole," he says. "You think I'm fucking stupid. You think I can't tell."

"Can't tell what, what the fuck are you talking about?"

"You, man." Frankie watches as the Escalade turns onto Clark and Frankie pulls up to the corner too, slows down to give the Escalade some space. Got to be a little extra careful when you're driving a bright red fucking car, little sporty car with a stupid loud ass tin can exhaust and all that, trying to be inconspicuous.

Frankie continues: "You're sitting here all fucking day falling asleep. You can't sit still. You're sweating even though there's ice on the windows. You're whining about every little thing like a fucking bitch." Frankie shakes his head. "You motherfucker. I know what you're doing."

"I'm—"

"You're using again, I know you are. I got fucking eyes and I've known you long enough to know."

"I'm not, I'm—"

Up ahead the Escalade slows down and turns into a narrow alley, barely wide enough for the big ass SUV to fit through and Frankie pulls over half a block away.

"Shut the fuck up for a second," he says, then he stares out through the windshield at the opening to the alley.

Dildo shifts in his seat. He wipes at the sweat running free down his forehead. His skin feels sticky. He either wants to be sick or die or just fix up real quick to get himself right.

He just wants a taste. One little taste of what he's got chilling in his pocket, waiting for him when he's done here with Frankie. One taste and everything can be easy and cool again.

"Look," he says. "Can I—"

"I said *shut the fuck up a second*." And he's still staring out the windshield.

Dildo looks over at the opening to the alley too. "Shouldn't you like, I don't know—are we going to lose him just sitting here?"

He points at the alley.

"No way out through there," Frankie says.

The alley leads to a small parking lot behind the dark little building.

"He not going anywhere for a while anyway," Frankie says. He leans his seat back a bit, tries to get comfortable as best he can in the tiny space.

"How do you know?"

Frankie scratches at the stubble on his face. He closes his eyes, says: "Every Friday, right around this time, say

68

three o'clock or so, this motherfucker drives his Escalade over to this little building, he parks around back, goes inside, and then he pays the lady in there to suck his dick and put a few fingers up his ass while she's down there doing her thing."

"Well—what?" Dildo says. He wasn't expecting that. "I mean, how do you know all that?"

"What do you mean *how do I know all that*? It's my fucking job to know all that. Supposed to be your fucking job to know all that too," he says. "Plus, I mean everyone fucking knows that, right? You really going to sit there and tell me you didn't know that?"

"I mean...I don—"

"That's the problem, though, right? That you don't know. And you don't know because you're a fucking retard, is why."

Dildo doesn't say anything to this. He keeps looking out the window.

"You think people don't see you out here fucking around like this. You think people don't know. You're using again and there's going to come a time when you fuck something up, or do something stupid—like you always do when you're using—and then the next thing you know, one day it's going to be someone else sitting out here in a car while you go inside some place to do whatever. Get your dick sucked, shoot some dope, take a fucking shit. Whatever. They'll be sitting right out here, watching you walk in so that they can meet you with a gun to your face when you come walking back out again."

Dildo takes a deep breath. Doesn't know what to say, so what he does say is: "I mean...it's not—"

Frankie looks at Dildo, says: "You ain't got to say

69

shit. I know. We've known each other our whole lives and that's all I'm saying. You know?"

And they're quiet again for a few minutes. Because there's nothing else to say. Frankie's said his piece and Dildo's just Dildo. He'll either hear the thing or he won't. They don't call him Dildo for nothing.

After a while Dildo says: "So what the fuck are we doing now?"

Frankie shrugs. "We're just waiting, I guess."

"But like why don't we go in there and do him now?"

"Fuck, man. Let the guy get his nut off before we do him like that."

"Fuck that. Let him finish? For what?"

"We're getting paid to make him dead. That don't mean we got to be dicks about it."

And Frankie's serious. Figures they're going to kill the fucking guy anyway. Why not let him finish doing his thing in there first? Let him get whatever he can get before they send him wherever he's going.

After about twenty minutes Frankie nods at Dildo and they both get out of the car. They walk around through the little alley to the back of the building and lean against the Escalade while they wait.

Dildo sparks up a cig now that he's outside and away from Frankie's bullshit no smoking in the Honda rule. He closes his eyes while he takes that first drag and when he's finally breathing out again he says: "Look man, I know I been fucking up but I'm really go—"

The building's back door opens and Frankie tells Dildo, "Shut the fuck up."

The guy steps out, but he's still looking back over his shoulder, talking to someone inside.

Frankie pulls the gun out of his pants and steps up to

meet the guy at the door, points the piece so it's right between his eyes when he finally turns to face the alley.

"I hope it was a good one," Frankie says.

"Wh—what?" the guy says. He's staring straight at the gun and it's got him shook. Coming out of a building like that, after doing what he was just doing in there, not expecting there to be a gun waiting for him.

"I hope it was a good one," Frankie says again. "The blowjob and all them fingers up your ass, I was just saying that I hope it was a good one."

And then Frankie pulls the trigger and shoots the guy right in the forehead.

"Fuck, man," Dildo says after a few seconds.

Frankie's still looking at the guy. Like he thinks he might not be fully dead yet. Ready for him to spring back up.

"What?" Frankie finally says, turning back toward Dildo.

"I mean...that whole thing was...I don't know."

"Fucking badass, is what you mean."

"What?"

"The saying, all that, how I did him," Frankie says. "I been practicing that line for like the last twenty minutes."

Dildo shrugs.

"It *was* badass though," Frankie says.

"I am going to get clean again," Dildo says. Kind of out of nowhere. "I know I need to."

"Fuck you," Frankie says. "Like I ain't heard that before."

"But I am—"

"Fuck you," Frankie says again. He points at the guy's body lying there in the alley. Tells Dildo: "Grab his fucking wallet while we're just standing here because fuck him too."

He shrugs and starts walking back toward the Honda. Dildo grabs the guy's wallet, cell phone, lighter, cigs, watch, whatever else he can get his hands on, and Frankie calls over his shoulder: "I can give you a minute if you need to, you know, necrophilia all over him or whatever."

Daniel Vlasaty is the author of The Church of TV as God, Amphetamine Psychosis, Only Bones, A New and Different Kind of Pain, *and* Stay Ugly. *He lives outside of Chicago with his wife and daughter.*

Painkiller

By Wilson Koewing

Jason Walker opens his eyes. A heart monitor beeps. Tubes run from his wrists, nose, and mouth. Harsh light assaults his eyes. A doctor blurs into view.

"Mr. Walker, you've been through quite an ordeal. Your carotid artery was severed by a bullet. That bullet is still inside your head, pushing against the artery, holding it together. Remarkably, it's the only thing keeping you alive."

"Where are my daughters?"

"I don't know," the doctor says. "There's a detective here."

The doctor leaves. The detective approaches.

"I'm Detective Drake."

"My daughters?"

"We don't know yet," Drake says. "Mr. Walker, do you have any idea who might have done this? Do you have any enemies?"

"Enemies?" Jason says. "No, I'm an architect."

"What about your wife?"

"My wife's dead."

73

"I know that," Drake says. "I'm sorry. Did she have any enemies?"

"I don't know."

"What did your wife do?"

"She ran a nonprofit that advocated for affordable housing."

"I'm sorry to be blunt, Mr. Walker," Drake says, "but someone shows up at your front door, shoots your wife, then shoots you, and you know nothing?"

"It's all blank."

"If you remember anything give me a call."

Drake hands Jason his card and leaves.

As the door closes, Jason sees Drake approach a man he recognizes as one of the gunmen. Seeing his face, the events of the night flood back.

* * *

Jason chases his young daughters, Lilly and Paige, around the living room. Paige holds a Barbie. His wife, Alice, stands by the kitchen island drinking wine, preoccupied with her phone.

"Honey, how long ago did you order the pizza?" she asks.

"Should be here any minute!"

Jason labors into the kitchen holding the wriggling girls.

"Everything okay?" Jason asks.

"The other bidder on the lot is trying to bully us out of the deal."

"Don't worry, honey," Jason says. "It will work out."

"I don't know," she says. "These people are relentless."

The doorbell rings.

"I'll get it," Alice says, heading toward the front door.

The girls cheer the pizza's arrival.

A shotgun blast rings out. Jason turns toward the sound. Paige's Barbie falls to the ground. Alice's wineglass shatters.

Jason pushes the girls behind the bar and sprints to the foyer.

A masked gunman runs into him. They struggle.

Jason is able to pull off the gunman's mask before the butt of a shotgun knocks him out.

When Jason comes to, Paige and Lilly are tied up and being forced to watch. A combat boot is to his throat. The gunman points a pistol and fires a bullet into Jason's brain.

* * *

Jason disconnects the tubes and gets dressed. His head is covered with a thick bandage.

He peeks out of his hospital room. He waits for the elevator. He approaches a nurse's station on a different floor.

"Can you help me?" Jason says. "I've forgotten the doctor's instructions."

"Of course," a nurse says. "What's your name?"

"Jason Walker."

The nurse accesses his file.

"I understand why you forgot," she says. "You should be in bed, Mr. Walker."

"I have to get out of here."

"One moment," she says entering a room behind the nurse's station.

Jason waits nervously.

The nurse returns with a bottle of painkillers.

"Take these as needed for pain," the nurse says. "You need water and rest, Mr. Walker. You're in a delicate state. Any head trauma and you could die instantly."

She scans Jason's file, growing more concerned.

Jason is gone.

He staggers away from the hospital and pops a painkiller. He stumbles into a gas station and grabs a water. He approaches the cashier.

"Three bucks."

Jason searches his pocket for his wallet, but it isn't there. He looks up at the cashier with crazed eyes then falls, knocking over a display.

The cashier rushes around the counter and helps him up.

"Just take the water, man."

* * *

Police tape covers the door of Jason's home. He kicks at it, but it won't budge, so he crashes through with his shoulder. The house is trashed. He grabs his wallet from his drafting table then hears the beep of an incoming text. He looks around, confused. He finds his wife's phone on the bookshelf, just out of sight.

He's forgotten her passcode but can see a message from an unnamed number on the notifications screen: *We're getting that lot one way or another, Mrs. Walker.*

Before he leaves, Jason rips a family portrait from the wall, breaks the glass, grabs the photo, and puts it in his pocket.

* * *

Jason stands at an ATM. A wheel spins on the screen as his request processes. The machine spits out bills that Jason stuffs in his pocket.

Jason stalks the city streets. Seedy bars, strip malls. Detroit remains in sharp decline. Undesirables litter sidewalks and alleys.

He approaches a twenty-four seven pawn shop glowing dull in the distance.

A bell dings as he enters. Fluorescent lighting. The city squeezes in from the outside.

A clerk stands behind a glass case of knives and handguns.

"I need a gun," Jason says.

"Will any gun do?" the clerk snickers.

"That one." Jason points at a snub nosed .38.

The clerk produces forms and places the .38 on the case.

"Fill these out," the clerk says. "Obviously there's a waiting period."

Jason grabs the .38.

"That's not going to work."

"This isn't that kind of place."

"Don't you have anything for someone who...doesn't want to fill out paperwork?"

Jason places cash on the counter.

"Sir, I can't help you. Now get the fuck out before I bash you one."

"Listen, shit bird," Jason says. "You see this bandage?"

"Yeah."

"Doorbell rang, wife answered, shotgun blast," Jason says. "Before I knew it, there's a bullet in my brain."

Jason grabs the clerk by the collar and pulls him

close. "And it's still in there."

The clerk pushes Jason back.

"Sad story, friend."

"I'm leaving with a gun, one way or another."

Jason pushes the .38 to the clerk's forehead.

The clerk cocks a shotgun and points it at Jason's stomach.

"Mine's loaded," the clerk says.

Jason pulls the trigger. The clerk flinches but doesn't fire the shotgun. Jason drops the gun on the counter. His gaze is drawn to a jet-black motorcycle helmet on a shelf.

"How much for that helmet?"

* * *

Jason walks across the parking lot carrying the helmet.

"Hey, you," the clerk stands in the doorway holding out a card, "Call this number, mention the clerk."

Jason calls the number.

"Yeah?"

"The clerk said to call."

"Fifteen, Old Park Way. Come alone."

* * *

A cab driver's eyes dart between the road and Jason.

"Fifteen, Old Park Way?" the cab driver asks suspiciously.

Jason glares at him.

"Prick," the cab driver says under his breath.

Jason watches the passing streets. Cold concrete. Dark figures in shadows. Decrepit buildings. Barrel fires.

The cab drops Jason outside of a run-down warehouse. The giant brick void melds into the night. Broken windows reflect dim moonlight. Downed power lines dangle over puddles.

Jason moves through shadows. Water drips from pipes. He ascends stairs, navigates a dark hallway, and enters a makeshift living area in the middle of a large open space. A mangy mutt lies before a wood burning stove.

A hulking man places various pistols on a table. They look like toys in his hands.

The mutt growls.

"He doesn't like you," the hulking man says.

"I need a pistol."

"You get right to the point."

He hands Jason a .38 snub nose.

"Deadly at close range, accurate enough from mid," he says. "Won't jam on you and you get off five shots pretty quick."

Jason awkwardly holds the gun.

"Accountant?"

"Architect."

Jason spins the chamber.

The hulking man hands Jason a box of bullets. He loads several backwards.

"Might want to turn those around."

Jason loads the bullets properly, then flicks his wrist and the chamber locks.

"How much?"

"Your money is no good here."

Jason stares at the gun in his hand.

"The other cot is yours if you need a place to stay," the hulking man says before disappearing into the shadows.

Illuminated by the fire from the wood-burning stove,

Jason climbs in the cot. He pulls out the family portrait and gives himself over to sleep.

* * *

Jason arrives at his wife's nonprofit office and peers through the door. Not a soul. Her death must have afforded everyone a vacation. He covers his hand with the sleeve of his jacket and punches the glass. The door shatters.

Jason enters the office and sees *Alice Walker* on a placard. Family photos. Overtaken, he sweeps everything from the desk onto the ground with his arm.

Gathering himself, he notices a newspaper clipping taped to the computer monitor.

Jason reads the article: *Local real estate magnate Dalton Westlake to bring designer fashions and high-end boutiques to central city as small businesses/proposed affordable housing projects fall by the wayside*.

* * *

Glass bottles are lined up deep in the bowels of the abandoned warehouse. Jason readies to fire. The hulking man watches, polishing a gun. Jason fires off a round. Hits nothing.

"Reload, what are you waiting for?" the hulking man says.

Jason reloads. Fires off another round and again hits nothing.

"Pull, don't squeeze."

Jason reloads, fires, and misses.

"Again."

Jason reloads, fires off two shots, hits nothing, drops the gun to his side.

"Aim at each bottle then close your eyes," the hulking man says.

Jason begrudgingly aims at each bottle then closes his eyes.

"On the count of three, shoot the bottles," he says. "One, two, three."

The hulking man fires in unison with Jason, the bottles explode one by one.

Jason opens his eyes, amazed.

"You're ready."

* * *

Jason eats noodles from a pot listening to the rhythmic scraping of a brush against steel. Fire crackles in the stove. The hulking man cleans a gun.

"Dalton Westlake is a powerful man," he says.

"A powerful man with answers," Jason says.

"How can you be so sure?"

"It's all I've got."

"I had a wife once, too,"

"Let me guess," Jason says, "she didn't think this was a suitable place to raise a family?"

"Murdered," he says. "Couldn't get me, so they took what was most important to me."

"What did you do?"

"I killed my pain away."

* * *

Jason stares up at a skyscraper.

Through the floor-to-ceiling windows, he watches security guards usher visitors through metal detectors.

He wanders around the building until he finds an alley to hide his gun in.

Past security, he finds Westlake Real Estate Group on the building map. The elevator climbs to the fortieth floor. The floor is plush. An intricate fountain. A lone receptionist behind a desk.

"Dalton Westlake," Jason says.

"Do you have an appointment?"

"I don't."

"No one sees Mr. Westlake without an appointment."

"I'm curious about his current projects," Jason says. "I'm a fan of the mall job."

"Oh, are you an investor?"

"Yes."

"Mr. Westlake provides a portfolio for potential investors," she says. "It chronicles current projects and future plans."

"I'd love to see his plans for the future."

The receptionist produces a folder.

"What happened?" she says, referring to Jason's bandage.

"I was shot in the head."

Jason smiles at the shocked secretary and leaves.

***

Jason steps out of the elevator into the lobby. A man brushes past. Jason catches a glimpse.

It's the masked gunman.

Jason follows him outside into the streets. He stops at a newspaper stand. Jason sprints down the alley to retrieve his gun.

Emerging back into the street, there's no sign of the gunman. Jason turns a corner and spots him climbing into a black Chrysler.

Jason hails a cab.

The Chrysler turns down an alley. Jason watches the gunman enter a shop and return with two briefcases.

The cab follows the Chrysler through traffic. Eventually it stops at a gentleman's club.

Jason follows the gunman inside.

"Wait here," he tells the driver.

Inside, lights flash, illuminating dark figures. Music blares. Women dance and offer lap dances.

Jason notices the gunman slink behind a curtain.

A woman approaches Jason. "What's your name?"

He ignores her.

"Well fuck you."

Jason sits at a table. A cocktail waitress approaches.

"What can I get you?"

"I'm fine."

"There's a one drink minimum."

"I'll have a water."

"There's a one alcohol drink minimum."

"Doesn't matter," Jason says.

Jason watches her whisper to a bouncer and point in his direction.

She returns with a rocks glass.

"What is it?"

"J&B," she says. "Looks like you could use it."

Jason takes a long sip. His vision blurs. He pops a painkiller. The music pulses. The dancers. The faces of the men. Money floating in the air. Strobe lights. It all blends together, making Jason woozy.

He snaps out of it, noticing the gunman scurrying out.

Back in the cab. Rush hour. Jason watches passing cars. People heading home from work. Families. Everyone in a hurry.

The Chrysler slices through slow traffic just ahead.

"Don't lose him."

* * *

The cab pulls up to a construction site on the outskirts of the city. Two cronies with shotguns stand guard in front of a trailer. The Chrysler is parked outside. In the distance, the sun sets behind skyscrapers.

Jason observes from behind piles of construction materials, his head protected by the motorcycle helmet. He moves closer, taking cover behind a bulldozer before maneuvering to the side of the trailer, only a few yards from the cronies. He points his gun and steps into the open.

"Drop your guns."

"Who the fuck are you supposed to be?" one crony says.

Jason's finger slips on the trigger and blood splatters the trailer's wall and the helmet's visor.

Jason is shocked by what he's done.

He wipes at the visor, but it smears. He fires the gun wildly and misses. The crony tackles Jason to the ground. Grabs a steel pipe and swings it as Jason fires up. The crony staggers and falls, the empty space he leaves revealing the Westlake Real Estate Group skyscraper in the distance.

Jason rolls under the trailer and struggles to take off the helmet. The trailer door swings open and the gunman steps out. He picks up one of the shotguns.

"Come out," the man says. "Fight like a man, not a rat."

Jason scampers from under the trailer and takes out his legs. The shotgun slides away. In the melee, Jason drops his gun.

Jason jumps on the gunman and chokes him. The gunman knocks Jason off, landing a punch to the head. Jason stands wobbly. There's a moment of recognition from the masked gunman before he hurls a brick at Jason's head.

Jason ducks out of the way.

"You," he says. "Why wouldn't you die?"

The gunman dives for the shotgun. Jason tackles him. They struggle. The gunman gets free. He freezes hearing Jason's gun click. He's within reach of the shotgun.

"Why'd you do it?" Jason says.

"It's my job."

"Killing my wife?"

"No, scaring her was my job," he says. "Killing her was my pleasure."

Jason kicks the gunman under the chin and sends him rolling onto his back, but closer to the shotgun.

"You chose the wrong job."

"Fuck you," the gunman says, slowly reaching for the shotgun.

"Who sent you to my house?"

"It doesn't matter," he says. "You'll never get to him."

"Say the name."

"Go to hell."

Jason shoots a bullet into his thigh just as his hand reaches the shotgun. He screams out in pain.

"Say the name."

"You're going to die, you stupid bastard."

"Not before you."

Jason shoots him in the chest then stands over him, barely breathing, struggling to speak.

"Say it," Jason says.

"Dalton...Westlake..."

Jason deposits one more bullet in his brain, then searches him for a phone. He uses the guy's fingerprint to unlock it. Searches the contacts. He pops a handful of painkillers and starts walking. The phone rings in his ear.

A voice answers, "What is it?"

"Not what," Jason says. "Who?"

"Who the fuck is this?"

"The guy you should have finished off when you had the chance."

Jason hangs up and walks toward the black shadows and the steel trees of the concrete jungle. Hunting Dalton Westlake.

Wilson Koewing is a writer from South Carolina. His work is forthcoming at Hobart, Wigleaf, Oxmag *and* Gargoyle.

The Christmas Goose

By Tracy Falenwolfe

"Remember to prick the skin with a needle before you roast it." Heinrich Metzger gave all his regular customers who ordered a Christmas goose the same advice. What he really wanted to say was, If you don't already know that, you should have gone with a turkey, but he kept his mouth shut. His Lancaster, Pennsylvania butcher shop had seen a steep decline in business in recent years thanks to the vegans and the animal rights people and those hippies, the pescatarians, so he'd had to take on some side work for his old friend Steven Verba.

The work itself was simple, and he already had the equipment. Heinrich's cousins Willard and Carl Bauer owned pig farms adjacent to his own spread, which made it even easier. Usually. Today, though, Verba went and changed things up. He asked Heinrich to handle a special delivery, and Heinrich wasn't thrilled about it. It was three in the afternoon on Christmas Eve and the snow was starting to accumulate. He was open for another hour and there were still four orders to be picked up—one prime rib roast, two dressed turkeys, and another goose.

Three old, wise men were gathered in the corner of the shop. They were Heinrich's father's cronies, and after the local Grundsow lodge closed, they started congregating at the shop to buy their Lebanon bologna and speak Pennsylvania Dutch to each other. By law, Heinrich couldn't offer them a place to sit or the use of his restroom, but the men didn't care. Their only concern was that their language and traditions didn't die.

After Heinrich kicked them out for the day, they'd stand in the parking lot retelling the same stories, laughing at the same jokes, and carefully rolling up and eating one slice of smoked meat after the other until they'd worked their way through a whole pound.

The bells over the door jingled and Heinrich looked up. It was old lady Handwerk, come for her prime rib. She wanted some scrapple, and some chow-chow, and some hot bacon dressing too, now that she was here. Fine. Heinrich left her smaller items on the counter and went to the walk-in fridge for her prime rib. As he grabbed the roast he glanced down at Verba's special delivery on the bottom shelf. Wrapped in butcher paper like all of the other deliveries, it was the same general shape and weight of a goose. It didn't strike Heinrich earlier, when he'd been in the cooler for the Dietrichs' turkey, but now that he looked again, the gold Metzger's sticker and the red and green plaid bow and the compliments of Steven Verba gift tag stood out like a string of flashing lights.

Heinrich's stomach turned. Verba's special delivery had no sticker, no ribbon, and no gift card, which meant Heinrich was looking at a regular old goose. His heart started drumming. If Verba's special package wasn't here, then where was it?

"Yoo-hoo?" old lady Handwerk stood at the counter and called. "You didn't give my prime rib to someone else, did you?"

If only he'd have been so lucky. Panicked, Heinrich hustled old lady Handwerk and the former lodge members out the door.

His long-time delivery person had quit last week after a stroke left him unable to drive, and Carl's son Garrett had been filling in. Heinrich loved his nephew, but the kid was a real waste case. He must have had Verba's package with him in the delivery van.

Heinrich's fingers shook as he dialed Garrett's number. The kid was always on his phone, so surely he would answer, but no. Heinrich texted instead. No response again.

He shed his apron and ran to his truck. The old wise men were still chewing in the parking lot. "*Was ist das?*" The eldest called out. "What's wrong, boy? It's not closing time yet."

"My nephew's out making deliveries and he took something he shouldn't have." Heinrich pulled on his coat as he spoke. "I have to find him and get it back."

"We can help," the old man said. "Whatever you need."

"*Ja,*" crony number two chimed in. "We helped your father all the time."

Heinrich wanted to say no thanks, but the faster he found Garrett, the better. The kid had made the customer deliveries before lunch. Since then he'd been delivering Christmas geese to local charities and soup kitchens. All the legit packages had been wrapped the same way— sealed with a gold Metzger's sticker, tied with a red and green plaid bow, and outfitted with a gift tag that said compliments of Steven Verba. How could Garrett have grabbed the unadorned package and not have noticed it was different?

Regardless, would Heinrich only be making things worse if he involved his father's friends in order to get it back?

He hesitated, eyeing the old men while he weighed his options. Not that he had many. Verba would flip if he ever found out what had happened, but he would be ruined if the wrong package was delivered to a charity on his behalf. He was a big deal in the community, and reputation meant everything to him.

Heinrich looked at the list again. He ripped it in half and gave the top to the elder crony. "He might be at one of these places. If you find him, stop him and tell him to call me."

Elder crony squinted at the list. He shook a cigarette out of a beat up pack of Camels and lit it. "These are all on the east side of the city, right?"

"Right."

The old guy nodded. "Let's go, then," he said to the others. "What are we waiting for? Christmas?"

The cronies were still cackling with laughter as Heinrich jumped into his truck. His head throbbed. He drove through the snow to the soup kitchen on Fourth Street where he pounded on the back door and rang the delivery buzzer. The priest who ran the place told him he'd missed Garrett by a matter of minutes, and that the goose he had delivered would feed many hungry mouths. Phew. He felt like a steer escaping the slaughterhouse.

The snow was picking up as Heinrich sped downtown to the second charity on his half of the list. Again, he had missed his nephew. Again, he was thanked for the goose.

Again, he thanked God that Garrett had gotten it right so far.

Jumping back into his truck, he vowed to hire a new delivery person, pronto. Then he said a silent prayer asking the powers that be to let him catch up to Garrett while Verba was still none the wiser. If he'd done the deliveries in order, the kid had only two more left. Hopefully he still had the plain package, because if it ended up in the wrong hands, all hell would break loose.

Heinrich tried calling and texting Garrett again, but got no response. He called Carl, who also didn't answer. Heinrich left a message outlining Garrett's screw up, and told Carl that if he heard from his son to tell him to stay exactly where he was and call Heinrich.

Heinrich's low fuel light lit up on the way to the third charity. It blinked a few times before glaring at him steadily. He coasted into a twenty-four-hour gas station and mini-market, and lo and behold, pulled up right next to his own delivery van. Garrett must have gone inside to use the bathroom or to get himself a snack, because he was nowhere in sight. Heinrich didn't even care. He considered it a Christmas miracle that his low fuel light had guided him to Garrett like the freakin' Star of Bethlehem.

Heinrich, praying for another miracle, approached the van, opened the door, and looked in the back. There it was—the plain package. The special delivery. Heinrich felt the contents through the paper, just to make sure. He'd wrapped it himself, but after losing track of it, he wanted to be doubly certain. Yup. A chill ran through him as he dragged his fingers over the paper. About the same shape and weight as a Christmas goose, but definitely not what's for dinner.

He slogged through the slush to take the package to his own truck. As he filled his gas tank, his phone rang. It was Steven Verba.

"Hello, Steven," Heinrich said. "What can I do for you?"

"Heinie." It was the nickname Verba had given him in grade school, as if there'd ever been a chance he'd be called something else. "We have a problem."

Heinrich swallowed, but knew not to speak.

"Your very eager delivery boy delivered a package to my home today. *My home.*"

Heinrich knew it still wasn't his turn to speak.

"Do you know what was in that package?"

Heinrich continued to bite his tongue.

"It was a Christmas goose, *from* me, meant for the homeless shelter by the river."

Bomb dropped. *Now* it was Heinrich's turn. "I'm sorry, Steven. That was my mistake. Keep the goose, I'll make sure the shelter gets another one, no charge. I'll deliver it myself."

"This is not about the goose, Heinie."

"I know." Heinrich swallowed. "I have the other package. I'm delivering it personally, right after I close the shop." He looked at his watch. "Don't worry, you can count on me."

"I'm not sure of that anymore."

"Look, the kid's my nephew. He's a stoner, I know it. But it's Christmas Eve, and the shop was busy and he must have just grabbed the wrong—" Heinrich realized he was listening to a dial tone. He didn't want to see Garrett right now, so he took off before the kid came back to the van and went to do what he had to do.

He was sweating bullets by the time he delivered the

plain package to Deuce Gelder. The tips of Heinrich's fingers tingled. He gagged once or twice on his way back to the van. No way to sugar-coat his sideline now. He was in it up to his giblets—no better than Verba, who'd sent the vile package as the result of a temper tantrum.

Verba was obsessed with rivalries. Every few months, he threatened to end their arrangement and take his business to Bob Klein, Heinrich's biggest competitor. Heinrich should have told him to go ahead and do that. Up until now, the job had been to chop up dead bodies and feed them to the pigs. Today, Heinrich handed a man his son's head in a plain brown wrapper. All because Gelder's son had come to work for Verba without mentioning who his father was, which had convinced Verba that the kid was a plant. Some kind of corporate spy.

Heinrich heard Gelder's agonizing wail as he pulled away from the house. A few miles down the road he had to pull over and vomit in the snow.

Instead of going back to the shop, he drove to the cemetery behind the old Grundsow lodge and sat in the truck next to his father's grave. It was dusk, and red and green Christmas lights from the house across the street lit up the blanket of snow around the headstone. Heinrich's old man would be disappointed in him for sure. He'd been a butcher his whole life and had supported his family without ever having to do what Heinrich was doing. If he were still here, he'd be back at the shop swapping stories with his old lodge buddies. If he'd been hurting for money, he would have taken on a respectable side job, like shoveling manure or something.

Heinrich made up his mind then. After the holiday

he'd call Verba and tell him he was out. His cousins would be pissed about the extra money drying up, but that was too bad.

When he finally got back to the shop, the door was open and Bing Crosby was singing about silver bells. It sounded like a dirge.

Carl was behind the counter. Mr. and Mrs. Shoemaker were leaving with their turkey. "They were waiting in the lot when I got here," Carl said. "Where'd you take off to?"

"Long story." Heinrich rubbed his eyes. "Is Garrett back?"

"No, I haven't heard from him. That's why I came over. I've been trying to get in touch with him since you called." He looked uneasy. Worried for his son.

Heinrich recalled Deuce Gelder's wail and dry heaved.

"Whoa." Carl stepped back. "You sick?"

"I'll be okay." Heinrich pulled out his own phone and looked at it. "He hasn't gotten back to me either. Where the hell is he?"

The shop phone rang and Carl jumped on it. "Metzger's." He listened for a few minutes. "Uh-huh. Uh-huh." Then he shook his head. "Okay, I'll tell him."

"Garrett?" Heinrich asked as Carl hung up.

"No. Your dad's friends. They said to tell you they got a flat tire over on the east side somewhere. They've been wandering around looking for a phone to call a tow truck. They're going to get the tire fixed and head home."

Heinrich nodded.

Carl glanced into the lot. It was full dark now, and the snow was piling up. "I hope Garrett didn't have a wreck."

"I don't think he had a wreck. I think he got the

munchies and doesn't give a crap about making the deliveries."

"What's your problem today?" Carl asked.

Heinrich filled him in on the day's events, skipping the part where he threw up. "Tonight was the last time. I'm done. I'm sorry. We'll find another way to make some extra cash."

"You think it's going to be that easy?" The blood drained from Carl's face. "You think Verba will just let us stop?"

"Yeah," Heinrich said. "He doesn't really have a choice, does he?"

"Sure he does." Carl dragged his hands through his hair. He turned a circle. "He can choose to whack us both to keep us from going to the cops."

"With what?" Heinrich leaned against the counter and hung his head. "There's no evidence he ever did anything wrong. That was the beauty of the whole operation. No body, no crime."

"What if Gelder takes the head to the cops?"

"He won't," Heinrich said. "Guys like Verba and Gelder settle their own scores."

"I guess so," Carl said.

The bell above the door jingled, and Heinrich expected it to be Garrett or one of the customers he was still waiting for. Instead, a courier ran up to the counter with a package. It was wrapped in brown butcher paper and tied with a silver bow. The gift card on top said compliments of Steven Verba and Klein's butcher shop. It looked to be the shape and weight of a Christmas goose.

Since winning the Bethlehem Writers Roundtable Short

Story Award in 2014, Tracy Falenwolfe's stories have appeared in over a dozen publications including Black Cat Mystery Magazine, Spinetingler Magazine, Flash Bang Mysteries, *and* Crimson Streets. *Tracy lives in Pennsylvania's Lehigh Valley with her husband and sons. She is a member of Sisters in Crime, Mystery Writers of America, and the Short Mystery Fiction Society. Find her at TracyFalenwolfe.com.*

The Safe House

By Tom Leins

The elderly woman's face explodes in a ruptured mess of cartilage and bone as my lumpen forehead makes contact with the bridge of her nose. That's going to leave a fucking mark.

I wipe her blood out of my eyes and survey the wreckage. There are two men on the ground, bleeding from their broken mouths. Both punters, by the look of it. Cheap suits and rancid aftershave—the stink of which does little to mask their sweaty excitement at being in a suburban brothel on a Friday evening. Somehow, I don't think their night is turning out quite how they planned.

I spring off the heart-shaped bed and launch myself at the scrawny man in the black silk shirt, my brass knuckles connecting with the oily strands of hair plastered across his discoloured scalp. I wrench the knuckle-duster free of the greasy, bloody tangle and move towards the door. The screaming hookers are giving me a fucking headache.

I sidestep his co-worker—a fat motherfucker with a knuckle-knife—and the blade misses my heart as his fingers crunch into my elbow and the knife rips my jacket. I swivel sharply and force the same elbow into his jawbone. It connects with a satisfying crunch of busted teeth. I sweep his legs for good measure and his chubby head hits the doorframe. One madam and two security guards, Malinquo told me. Job done.

I beckon to the girl, Barbie, and she peels herself off the far wall and tiptoes through the carnage. She was easy to find. The only black girl in the brothel. I rip a satin sheet off the nearest bed and pass it to her, to wrap herself in. Like everything else in the room, it reeks of stale semen and old cigarette smoke.

We're halfway down the dimly-lit corridor when I feel the gun barrel against the back of my shaven skull.

"Hey motherfucker, kiss the ground."

I nod and lower myself towards the linoleum. I launch my right boot backwards into the space where one of his knees should be and my heel makes contact with a sick crack. The triggerman lands on me with a grunt, his gun discharging into the corridor wall. I wriggle out from under him and stamp on his wrist, kicking the gun towards the lobby. He's a big bastard—looks like he could do a lot of damage to a man like me.

Sure enough, he springs to his feet and assumes a boxer's stance. Younger, taller and healthier than me, he lets rip with a jab-hook-uppercut combo that snaps my head back and leaves me smeared across the corridor wall. He chuckles sourly—presumably anticipating a better fight—and edges closer.

"Fuck this."

I learned a long time ago not to leave blood, phlegm or semen at a crime scene, but that won't be possible today.

I spit blood in his eyes and sidestep his right hook. I double him over with a punch to the gut and drive my knee into his face. Once. Twice. Three times.

Barbie is trembling in the lobby, the satin sheet still wrapped around her scrawny body. I retrieve the Glock from the lino for safekeeping and tuck it down the back of my jeans.

"Come on. Let's go."

My skull throbs, and I feel my right eye swell up. I push Barbie in front of me and she wobbles on the uneven pavement in her transparent heels, so I grab her elbow to steady her. I raise my hood and keep my eyes directed at the pavement, cautious to avoid any unexpected CCTV entanglements. We walk for at least ten minutes, switching direction every two streets.

We're on a suburban street I don't recognise. A small strip of boarded-up retail units with deserted-looking flats above them. I see a bus stop with shattered windows and a concrete bench seat and tell Barbie to sit down. I've no idea if she knows what's going on, because she looks more nervous than she did back in the brothel.

I remove the mobile phone that Malinquo gave me from my shredded jacket. It's a late '90s Nokia, the kind drug dealers favour for the battery life. I dial the saved number with a bloody forefinger, leaving crimson fingerprints all over the handset. The machine picks up with a robotic click. I say nothing, like Malinquo told me—just wait twenty seconds and then hang up.

I blink away the rain, feeling woozy.

I try to fight the wave of tiredness and nausea that washes over me. Next to me, Barbie feels angular as she shivers uncontrollably.

I drift in and out of consciousness, unsure how much

time has passed, when I'm blinded by full-beam headlights at the end of the road. Malinquo's driver, I hope, as I'm in no fit state for another ruck.

I feel the tell-tale bulge of his shoulder holster against my ribcage as he heaves me onto the back seat of the hatchback. His face is stubbled and his aftershave reminds me of the ruined men in the brothel.

The last thing I remember is Barbie's smile. She looks relaxed for the first time since we met.

When I was hired, I was told that she was West African. Trafficked into the country by one of Malinquo's associates, only to end up in the wrong venue, in the wrong fucking town.

"Unless you have a basic grasp of French, don't waste energy trying to strike up a conversation," I was told.

It might be the delirium, but when she greets the driver, it sounds like she has a fucking Bristolian accent.

Blood. Piss. Pain. Chaos. Welcome to my world.

I pass out before we reach the end of the street.

* * *

Six hours later

It was an extraction. Nothing more, nothing less. I've rescued dozens of girls from dozens of brothels over the last decade, and the jobs pay well with minimal blowback. Occasionally, months or years later, I bump into a familiar face in a pub. Either a working girl, or a punter, or a bouncer, but they always blink first and look away—remembering the havoc I wreaked during our brief acquaintanceship.

Malinquo was a new client, but the job sounded legit, and he offered double my going rate—payment upfront. The money, address and phone were handed to me in the car park of a derelict pub by his driver, a thickset cliché with an unbranded bomber jacket and a freshly shaved head. Again, not particularly unusual. Men with dirty secrets like to obscure their business interests with middle-men and subterfuge, to ensure deniability. Malinquo didn't seem too different.

Now, I find myself propped against the corrugated iron wall of a barn, staring at the morning rain. The barn is mercifully empty: no animals and no animal shit. Across the concrete courtyard is a dilapidated farmhouse. There's an unsteady-looking pile of half-rusted appliances in one corner of the yard and a skip full of rubble a few feet from the front door.

On the floor next to me are a bottle of Happy Shopper mineral water and a Mars bar. The seal on the bottle looks like it's been tampered with. I unscrew the lid and sniff the contents. Despite the lack of smell, I toss it aside. I haul myself off the floor and shake some life into my aching limbs. I check my jeans for the Glock, but it's been removed, as has the mobile phone. Weirdly, a four-digit code has been written on the back of my left hand with marker pen.

My throat is parched, so I walk across to the far end of the barn, remove the rotten length of hose pipe attached to the stand pipe, twist the handle and drink thirstily from the cold trickle. Then I eat the Mars bar and try to take in my surroundings. Apart from the farmhouse, there's not another building for miles. As far as my bloodshot eyes can see.

Even if there was, the boggy terrain and lashing

rain dissuade me from attempting to flee the scene. I'm assuming I'm somewhere on Dartmoor, or down in Cornwall—places I can navigate my way home from— but I was out cold for long enough to be almost any-where in the UK. I take another drink from the tap and piss in the corner of the barn. My urine is dark yellow. Dehydrated, but no blood, which is something, at least.

I stare at the farmhouse. I've been dumped here for a reason, and whoever—or whatever—is waiting inside for me feels as inevitable as a bullet.

I stare at the building a moment longer, noticing the bricked-up windows, then start to walk across the courtyard.

I'm not a man resigned to my fate. Fuck, no. I look fate in the eye and I don't fucking blink.

* * *

The thick oak door looks ancient, but it has a brand-new, high-tech lock affixed to it. So new, in fact, I can still see traces of sawdust and wood shavings on the ground in front of the porch. I double check the four digits that the driver wrote on the back of my hand and prod them into the adjacent keypad. The heavy door unlocks with a mechanical click, and I heave it open and step into the small porch.

Less than ten feet away, there's a metal detector in front of the next door. It's not a new model—its white casing is grubby with age, and the equipment looks rudimentary, like the kind of kit you'd find in a regional airport. The laminated, handwritten sign sellotaped to the machine says 'No Weapons Allowed'.

My brass knuckles were removed along with the gun, so I step through the machine, which emits a brief, shrill warning. I step back and remove the pig-knife from my boot, dropping it in the wheelie bin and pass through the metal detector—and the door behind it. Metal sheeting this time, like the kind used to keep vagrants out of abandoned buildings.

I brace myself for punches, kicks, maybe a lump of masonry aimed at my skull, but all I see are three defeated-looking middle-aged men, sat on ratty mattresses against the back wall.

A man with a doughy face and a receding hairline hauls himself off his mattress. Apart from his fleshy features, he looks pretty solid. Tall, with a slight gut. His white shirt is grimy, so he must have been here for some time.

"Welcome to the fucking party, son."

Then the metal door slides back into place behind me.

* * *

He edges closer, but not too close. Even from ten feet away he stinks like an unrefrigerated corpse.

"You got any ciggies, new boy?"

I shake my head.

"Don't smoke, mate. Smoking can kill you."

He grunts and paces the perimeter, shaking his head with irritation. I recognise him from somewhere, but I'm not sure where. When you've been punched in the face as often as I have, a blast from the past needs to have the velocity of a fucking shotgun blast to snag my attention.

I turn towards my other two companions. The second

figure isn't a man at all, but a woman with a shaved head, a faded army surplus jacket—and a gangrenous looking stump where her left foot should be. Up close, she's grubby, but pretty, with prominent cheekbones and large, bruise-coloured lips. A thick pink scar traverses her stubbled hairline.

The last man looks up briefly and scowls at me through his unruly black beard. He spits on the ground distastefully, crossing his arms over his chest, without saying a word. He's swaddled in a thick, garishly-patterned robe that reminds me of the carpets you used to be able to buy on Winner Street in the '80s and '90s. He looks Middle Eastern, but it's hard to tell.

"What the fuck is this place?"

The big man grinds to a halt, seemingly pleased by the question.

"It's a safe house, son, but not one I've ever seen on the books—which pretty much rules out Devon and Cornwall."

"Hold up, mate. 'On the books'? Are you a fucking cop?"

He nods. "DS Robert Southern. Bobby to my mates. Seventeen years on the job. Currently suspended on full pay, pending an, erm, inquiry."

The woman clears her throat. "Our sloppy friend here was caught stealing drugs and guns from the evidence locker at Charles Cross nick on behalf of Mr fucking Malinquo."

The big man frowns. I step towards him.

"The only thing worse than a cop is a bent fucking cop."

He stands his ground, juts out his chest, his jaw, breathing heavily through his nose.

I feel my fists clench, then I step back from the brink.

"Hold up: you two know Malinquo too?"

They both nod.

The girl is the first to speak: "Unfortunately, we do."

* * *

Bobby Southern leans against the far wall, trying to spark up a cigarette butt he found on the floor.

"To say I know him is overstating the case, son. He paid me to retrieve certain incriminating items on his behalf and fixed me up with this safe house while he sorted my new passport and papers. That was...what day is it now?"

"Saturday."

He puffs gamely on the dog-end and counts using his fingers.

"Eight fucking days ago."

Fuck me.

"Who has been here the longest? You?"

He nods. "Me first. Then fucking stumpy, then laughing boy, now you."

I stare at him. He looks shifty.

"First man in, last man out, right? Sounds like maybe you orchestrated it, Southern. Veteran cop. Friends in high places. Time to settle some scores before you check out. What is it? Terminal illness? Something eating away at your bones? Your insides? Getting in God's good books before you shuffle off this mortal coil, are you?"

He scoffs and turns away. Abruptly, he pivots and slams his right fist into my jaw, knocking me off my feet and leaving me leaking blood.

The girl laughs nastily, and I shuffle backwards on

my arse, in case Southern wants a second helping.

"I've told you my truth, son. Now you tell me yours. Who the fuck are you, anyway?"

I consider what I should tell them. I was an unlicensed private investigator for many years, but the rules of the game were starkly defined, and that line of work never really suited me.

I wipe my bloody lips on my sleeve.

"I do jobs for people. The kind of jobs no one else wants to do."

He clicks his fingers. "You're Rey right? Joe Rey?"

I nod and he grins unpleasantly.

"I had to clean up after that little clusterfuck with the Grinley Family down at Marsh Mills." He whistles through his teeth. "That was a real number you did on those inbred bastards. Of course, we pinned it on the fucking Albanians. Any excuse to roust those dirty fuckers!"

I massage my jaw. It feels like it might be broken.

"Sure. That's me. Nice to know that my reputation precedes me. Always nice to meet a fucking fan…"

He smiles, big hands on his hips. "Well, I suppose there are worse people to be locked in a fucking safe house with. Right stumpy?"

She flashes him a middle finger. "Fuck off, Sarge."

She closes her eyes and leans her head back against the stonework. "My name's Zula Hook, and yeah, I know Malinquo too."

* * *

Zula tells us that she was a professional kickboxer—until she lost her fucking foot.

In her owns words, she was an also-ran—constantly coming up against bigger, quicker, tougher opponents. A disgraced ex-trainer suggested she should use Oradexon to help her bulk up, stay competitive. Within six months, she was injecting the shit between her toes daily. One bad batch from Bangladesh later, the foot went gangrenous, and actually burst during a fight. It was too far gone to save.

She sighs heavily. "A girl I used to knock around with, Geena, wanted to rip off one of the houses she cleaned at. A place in Riverside. Million-pound house. Easy pickings. I was depressed, drinking heavily—and didn't take much convincing to go in with her on a job. She said she would be the brains, I would be the brawn. I made it back to the car. She got nicked on the premises," she gestures to Bobby Southern, "by this shit stain and his mates. Geena went down for a five-stretch in Dartmoor, I walked."

"Or hobbled," Southern chuckles.

She scowls at him.

"A few months later, I was approached to steal an item from the same property. A solid gold cock ring, if you can believe it. I'm no thief, but I knew enough to disable the alarm and get in and out with a minimum of fuss."

"A thief stays a thief, unless she ends up in jail or dead," Southern scoffs.

Zula ignores him.

"I acquired the cock ring and dialled the number on the burner phone. The driver turned up to collect me, as arranged. Before I knew what was happening, there's a tranq dart in my neck and I woke up here, with the Sarge."

Bobby Southern smiles contentedly, hands still on his hips, and turns to face the guy with the beard.

"What about you, loud-crowd?"

The bearded man snorts dismissively. "I have never heard of this Malinquo that you speak of."

"Who the fuck are you?"

"Even my best friends don't know my real name. I certainly have no intention of discussing my past with common criminals like you."

Southern grunts. "Suit yourself, chuckles."

* * *

It's my turn to pace the room. I feel like a caged rat.

I trawl through my rolodex of pungent memories. How do I know these fucking people? How do they know me?

I stare at the thick scar across Zula's hairline, making no effort to conceal my curiosity. I recognise her. From the bareknuckle scene. She once beat a gypsy called Franky Elias at one of 'Mucky' Mickey Molloy's 'Bloody Knuckles' tournaments in the South Hams.

After the fight, Elias got drunk with his cousins and bounced her head off one of the concrete-filled oil drums that formed the four corners of the ring. She lost so much blood I assumed she had died.

I point to Southern's knuckles. They look smashed and misshapen.

"Are you a fighter, mate?"

He nods. "I've had a few scraps."

"Bareknuckle?"

"Once or twice. If the price was right."

"You ever work one of Mucky Mickey's tournaments?"

He nods. "Once. Or twice."

Then the slow clap starts.

"I knew I could count on our private eye friend Mr Rey to unravel this little mystery! Truly, he's not as dumb as he looks!"

The Middle Eastern inflection is gone, replaced with a smoother, more formal accent. A tone more suited to boardrooms than addressing bastards like me. He lowers his hood. His nails are manicured, his hair a neatly trimmed side-parting.

"You are truly wasted brutalising brothel-keepers, Mr Rey."

I stare at him in disbelief.

"You? You're fucking Malinquo?"

Zula struggles to her feet and joins us, standing over him.

"As I have already informed you: not even my best friends know my real name."

Southern moves closer to Malinquo, his big, veiny fists tensing. He spits on the ground and looms over the seated man. Surreally, Southern starts reading him his rights:

"I am arresting you on suspicion of kidnapping. You do not have to say anything, but it may harm your defence if you do not mention when questioned something you later rely on in court. Anything you do say may be given in evidence."

Malinquo—or whatever the motherfucker's name is—shakes his head and withdraws a gun from the folds of his ugly robe, placing it against Bobby Southern's rubbery jowls. He pulls the trigger and the bent cop's face explodes like a melon that's been dropped off a multi-storey car-park.

"I have nothing in common with you fucking people," he shouts—to no one in particular.

* * *

I back off, careful not to tread in the bloody halo forming around Bobby Southern's bullet-shattered skull.

"Don't be shy, Mr Rey. You weren't backwards in coming forwards on twentieth June last year."

I scratch my head.

"I'm sorry, mate, I don't follow."

Malinquo grimaces. "That afternoon you participated in 'Bloody Knuckles 15', an unlicensed boxing tournament organised by the late Michael John Molloy."

The late Mr Molloy? That's news to me.

"If you say so, mate."

"At the end of the fight, Mr Molloy orchestrated what I believe is termed a 'Battle Royale' for any inter-ested combatants. He had made more than ten thousand pounds on the betting action that day, and offered a bonus of a thousand-pound fee for the last man—or woman—still standing. Nine of the sixteen fighters were willing to take part."

Zula looks at me guiltily, but I have no idea why.

"During the next hour each one of you cretins inflicted life-changing injuries on my twenty-two-year-old son."

I stare at the floor.

I was ejected from the rumble by a career criminal named Snaith who almost busted my windpipe with a chokehold and kicked me face-first into the dead grass. Before that, I remember beating on a kid using my fists, elbows, knees. He was solidly-built, gym-toned, clean-cut.

He took the hits and he kept on coming.

"My son—my only son—wanted to become a mixed martial arts fighter. Naturally, I paid for the most experienced trainers, the best nutritionists, the finest physicians. In his first professional fight—on the undercard at a badly-promoted event in Plymouth—a rabid-looking Scotsman nicknamed 'Cerberus' detached his retina with an elbow to the face. My son was never allowed to fight professionally again, and within a year he was fighting on farmland with savages like you people. My son is now in a permanent vegetative state."

Malinquo raises his gun. "My revenge has been a long time in coming, Mr Rey, Ms Hook. It has been an elaborate operation, and I could have paid a small-town hitman to do the job just as well, but I wanted to look you all in the eye while you bleed out—just like I did with that rotten specimen, Molloy."

After the fight, when the kid was lying limp in the mud, I remember that Molloy offered anyone who was interested two hundred fifty pounds if they could throw the unconscious body over his static caravan. The man I now know as Bobby Southern tried twice, before putting his back out. I still remember the sound the meaty body made as it crunched into the aircon unit on the side of the caravan. After that, I walked away.

He points the weapon at my face, his eyes burning with fury. "Oh, fuck."

At that moment, Zula launches into an improbable roundhouse kick. Her stump judders into Malinquo's bearded jaw, and one of the rotten pustules on her diseased-looking ankle bursts, coating his beard in scummy-looking blood. The gun drops from his hand.

Malinquo struggles to his feet, a look of pure hate in

his eyes. "Revenge will be mine!"

I knock him out with one punch.

* * *

I rip apart the mattress with my bare hands and use the rancid fabric to gag Malinquo and bind his wrists and ankles. His eyes flicker open, so I kick his jaw like it's a football.

Zula sits on the concrete floor, tears in her eyes, blood-streaked pus oozing from her stump.

"You remember the kid?"

She nods.

"Me too."

She wipes her tears on her sleeve.

"No one forced him to be there that day. He was there of his own free will, and he was bigger than me, and bigger than fucking you."

"It's not right..."

"It never is, Zula. It never is."

"But..."

I shake my head, unwilling to discuss matters further.

"Hey, you still got your phone?"

She nods and unzips her army jacket, peeling off the white vest beneath. She looks embarrassed as she unfurls the bandages taping her breasts down. The bandage goes slack as it unravels, and the mobile phone falls loose onto the concrete. It's an old Nokia, just like the one I was given. I pick it up, locate the contacts section and dial the saved number. Same routine as before: I wait for the click, count to twenty, and then hang up.

"Ready?"

She nods.

"Let's go."

* * *

We have to use Malinquo's thumbprint to open the door to the lobby. I'm glad it's not a retina scan, as the mother-fucker is out cold, eyeballs rolled into the back of his skull.

I upend the wheelie bin. Zula removes her prosthetic from the small, pointless pile of criminal detritus and fixes it to her leg. I slip the pig-knife into my boot. Then we emerge blinking into the rain.

Zula retrieves a half-brick from the skip, adjusts her grip so that her fingers nestle in the groove. I root around until I find a suitable weapon. A length of rebar with an ancient lump of concrete attached. Easily capable of shattering a windscreen. Or a skull.

I glance across at her.

"You up for this?"

She nods and speaks through gritted teeth. "Whatever it takes."

We wait in silence. Less than an hour later we see headlights as the hatchback bumps down the rutted mud track towards the farmhouse.

Thick raindrops dance in front of the full-beam headlights.

Not for the first time, I look fate in the eye and I don't fucking blink.

Tom Leins is a crime writer from Paignton, UK. His books include Boneyard Dogs, Ten Pints of Blood *and* Meat Bubbles & Other Stories *(all published by Close to the Bone) and* Repetition Kills You *and* The Good Book: Fairy Tales for Hard Men *(both available from All Due Respect). His next book,* Sharp Knives & Loud Guns, *was published by All Due Respect in December. For more details, please visit*: https://thingstodoindevon whenyouredead.wordpress.com/.

The Jade Ring

By Preston Lang

The Jade Ring was sometimes called the poor man's *Maltese Falcon*. But this was ridiculous considering how many plot holes *Falcon* had, how hokey the score was, and how much tangier Ramona Dade was than cold Mary Astor. CJ spent a lot of time and energy trashing *The Maltese Falcon* even though she ranked it as the sixth or seventh best movie ever made. But *The Jade Ring* was two cuts above. Lean, mysterious, and beautiful, not a shot was wasted. Every scene ramped up the tension, and every line of dialogue crackled, spun, and surprised.

CJ had published eleven articles on *Jade*. The editor of *Noir Memories* suggested that she write about "a movie people have actually seen or care about." She dragged his carcass all over social media for months. After that, the only place that would still publish her was a small nonpaying monthly called *Gats, Gams, and Knuckles*. You could write *Bogart* five hundred times in crayon—they'd print it.

CJ would follow up on any scrap about *Jade*. She ran names and key phrases through every database she could find—the title, the stars, the creators. The director was a former cameraman from RKO named Victor Lugo who'd directed a few other films: uninspiring police dramas and a stilted circus picture. On *Jade,* though, Lugo held the camera straight and let the scenes play. What made it work was the script.

The screenwriter was an old army buddy of Lugo's named Frank Bauer. This was his only credit. CJ had once entertained the possibility that Bauer was a front for someone else, someone big—Faulkner, Trumbo, Dorothy Parker, Franz Kafka? But that wasn't it. The style was wholly unique, yet quintessentially noir. CJ wrote article after article about the depth and bite of the banter, the simple beauty of the early morning fog, and the women. All of them—complex, stylized, and acid-tongued, but real and sexy as hell.

When a huge trove of old police reports became available to the public in a searchable database, CJ jumped right on it and got a hit from Daneville, Iowa, 1946. A murder suspect used the old I-was-at-the-movies alibi. *Jade* had simply been dropped on a number of screens across America one Friday in October of 1946 as the B picture in a package with a musical called *Fancy Footin'*. No advanced information, no teasers in the trade magazines. The murder occurred the first night the movie had been shown publicly. The cops had the suspect write out the entire synopsis by hand. In 1946, this was a good alibi.

Criminal Report Daneville Police Department

I hereby submit the following report for
the day of October 26, 1946: The victim,

Al Harris, permanent residence unknown, was found strangled in the Oaktree Hotel on the night previous, October 25.

Suspect Dan Frieze interviewed on October 26. Suspect seen with victim by witnesses in the week before the murder. According Witness #1, suspect and Harris argued in public outside of hotel. On the night of October 25, Witness #2 saw a man believed to be Suspect enter Harris's hotel room at 7:30 PM and then leave at 9 PM or shortly after. Suspect claims he was at the movies from 7 PM until after 10:30 PM on the night of October 25.

A few pages were missing, and the cop's handwriting was cramped and hard to decipher, but the description of *The Jade Ring* was written in legible longhand by the suspect. He did a great job: the opening chase in the rain; Singapore Sam with a dagger in his boot; the delicious twist of the shoeshine boy's identity; all the double entendre about cave exploration; and the slowdance to frantic boogie-woogie piano. Then just before the conclusion...the murder of Ramona's sister.

Alone in front of her computer screen, CJ actually gasped. If you've seen the movie even once, you know the little sister does *not* die. She's got the last line of the movie—*Wouldn't catch me dead in a coat like that*. You might think, so what? The suspect made one mistake. But CJ knew what no other living soul knew: in the original screenplay, Ramona's sister *did* die, hit by a car in the desert just as the suspect had described. Three years earlier at a used bookstore in LA, CJ had lucked onto an original script. That yellowed stack of paper had been her holy grail. This now felt bigger.

The police had held the suspect overnight, but the next day they checked his alibi. The ticket seller at the theater remembered him. He'd bought one for the seven o'clock show. First he'd passed over a ten-dollar bill then realized he had thirty-five cents change in a back pocket. *Jade* came on before the feature. There might've been a few shorts or a news reel first, but if the suspect saw *The Jade Ring* that night, he couldn't have committed the murder.

CJ put on her gray double-breasted and a bias-cut, striped tie and drove west. Seventeen hours, away from her rented room and her minimum-wage job toward the Daneville town archives. There had to be more in the local papers, maybe even police reports that hadn't been put online. Over the years, CJ had learned that old midwestern towns never threw anything out. It wasn't always easy to find, but truth sat mute in boxes and folders. Rolling through America, CJ played favorite scenes in her head—Lydia scamming the shipping company with a slick badger game, Ramona leaning over the dying pianist, making him play "My Sweetheart's Smile." In no time, she'd arrived.

Daneville was one of those solid Iowa towns of just over thirty thousand that rise up modestly out of the corn centered around a cluster of honest stone buildings. CJ got in just after ten a.m. Town Hall was a short walk down Main Street. On the way, she passed the old movie theater. There was the box office where seven nickels would've let her live her dream—*Jade* on a real big screen. But on a cold Tuesday morning, it advertised a superhero sequel and that one with Hugh Jackman and a talking monkey. CJ combed her hair and straightened her tie in the reflection off the plexiglass.

* * *

The archivist was a small woman with a chipped front tooth. The nameplate on her desk read Audrey Tyne. Before CJ spoke a word, the archivist laughed lightly.

"Can I use the archives?"

"What for?"

"I'm a journalist, researching the Albert Harris murder."

"Never heard of it."

Her voice was tart and luscious.

"Happened in 1946, right here in Danville," CJ said. "I know my way around an archive, so I don't need any help."

"You don't need me to hold your hand?"

"Is there a fee?"

"No. Just leave your ID with me. But you can't smoke, and you can't eat anything too juicy."

"What's too juicy?"

"A pear, a plum, a peach."

Downstairs boxes were stacked to the ceiling, but it was well-organized, and CJ found the old newspapers right away. She had to fight a few cobwebs on her way to 1946, but the papers didn't crumble into dust when you touched them, and the print was still clear and easy to read. The *Bee* and the *Journal* both ran accounts of the murder almost daily.

The *Bee* wrote that Daniel Frieze, a salesman, had been brought in for questioning. The next day, he was no longer a suspect. CJ found Frieze's address in the

1946 phone book. He wasn't there in 1945 or 1947. From property records, she saw he was a renter. There was no mention of what kind of salesman he was or what business he had in town.

A week in, the police arrested and charged a mechanic named Joe Murphy. The victim's wallet had been found in a locker at Murphy's garage where Harris was having repairs done on his car. For a few days, Murphy claimed innocence. Then the papers started to describe the victim as a "suspected red," a "onetime member of subversive organizations," and "involved in deviant lifestyles." Soon after, Murphy confessed to the killing but claimed he was just defending himself from this strange little leftist.

It was getting good—a communist and a mechanic. In addition to being the best film ever made, *Jade* was also the most trenchant condemnation of capitalism ever put on screen. Some noirs attacked the concept of greed, but *Jade* indicted the whole rotten system. Without speeches or moralizing, it forced you to see the world in a different way.

Murphy got eighteen months for manslaughter. None of the papers ever mentioned the other suspect again— Frieze, the moviegoer. CJ was feeling giddy as she scanned residential listings near Frieze's residence where she found Peter Gordon, a two-year-old in the 1940 census. He'd lived across the street from the house Frieze had stayed in. He would've been eight when Frieze moved in. To CJ's surprise, he was still alive—a retired electrician living right where Frieze had left him in 1946.

It was past seven when CJ came up the stairs. The archivist had let her hair loose and set a bottle of rye on the counter.

"What time do you close?" CJ asked.

"Two hours ago."

"Sorry to keep you."

"If we stay open late, we all have to take one good pull."

She poured a generous tumbler for each of them

"Well, if those are the rules," CJ said.

"I don't make them, but I enforce them to the letter."

The bottle had a picture of a sketchy-looking gent in a powdered wig. The price-tag said 6.99, but it was damn good fire.

"Have you ever heard of a movie called *The Jade Ring*?" CJ asked.

"Solid B picture. Two car chases; one racy spelunking joke that snuck by the censors."

"You've really seen it?"

This girl was too good to be true.

"I looked you up, CJ." The archivist handed back her driver's license. "Eleven articles about this *Jade Ring*. I watched the whole thing while you were underground."

"It's great, isn't it?"

CJ lost her cool for just a second and flashed the big, deranged smile of an obsessive.

"What does it have to do with my archives?"

CJ gave her the whole story, ending with Peter Gordon.

"I know Pete," the archivist said.

"How well?"

"He botched the order for youth choir tee shirts, so my mom got him kicked out of church."

"What denomination?"

"Presbyterian. We'll be fine if we bring him a bottle."

They hit the liquor store for more rye and brought it over to Pete's place. The house was on the old side of the street, where all the homes were solid Victorian. On the other side, where Frieze's place had been, everything was prefabs with a gap before you got a convenience store and gas station.

Pete answered the door in a dress shirt and slacks.

"What do you want?"

"She's a reporter working on a story," Audrey said. "And she brought you whisky."

"I'm looking into the Albert Harris murder," CJ said.

"You know what her mother did to me?" Pete pointed to Audrey.

"Hey, don't pin that on me. I hate my mom more than you do. She broke her wrist in June, it was hilarious."

"Harris murder," Pete said.

"I was wondering about a man who lived across the street: Dan Frieze."

"That's a hell of a tie, young lady," Pete said to CJ.

It was a gift from a woman who told CJ only lies from day one. She said it had belonged to Cal Lafaro. Bit player in the '30s and '40s. In *Jade* he had a sad one-liner after he lost at dice in the casino scene. The tie did look a lot like his, but she knew it was fake. Still, she relished the naked deception.

"Can we come inside?" Audrey asked.

"Give me the bottle."

Pete's living room was filled with childish art and photographs of smiling kids, but he lived alone in the big house.

"They questioned Frieze about the murder," he said. "Then it turned out the big Irish guy did it. Got in a fight with that communist."

"You don't think Frieze was involved at all?"

"The Irish guy confessed, didn't he? He was out in

122

less than a year. Everyone was good to him, brought him their cars to fix. And I don't think he paid for another drink until the day he died."

"What do you remember about Frieze?"

"He had a woman who lived with him. But they weren't around much. They'd leave for weeks at a time. And, you know, they weren't married. They were chilling."

"Chilling?"

"Like kids today. My granddaughter, my niece, the girl who put in my cable TV. They just find a guy and—chill." He looked to Audrey. "Do you chill?"

"You know me, Pete: I don't go below simmer."

"What was the name of the woman who lived with Frieze?" CJ asked.

"Birgit. Name like a Viking's mistress. I've always remembered her. It was my mom who found out they weren't married. Goes up to the lady—how are you today, *Miss* Munsey. That Valhalla broad backhanded my mom into the street. We stayed away from her after that."

Something about the name Birgit landed with CJ—it tied in, but she couldn't remember how. Pete poured out half a glass for everyone, and Audrey raised her drink to the generous host.

"I can tell my mom to talk to the Rev," she said. "Maybe bring you back into the fold."

Pete shook his head.

"What do you get from religion? A few songs on Sunday and everlasting life?"

* * *

"Birgit Munsey," Audrey said at the Steel Toe Diner.

"Hell of a name for a lady who goes around smacking good Christian mothers."

She ate half a blueberry pie while CJ looked up the mystery woman. What she found was gold. Birgit was a minor figure in the American Communist Party starting in the mid-1930s. There she was in pictures with Earl Browder and Paul Robeson—short, neat hair, and a long modest skirt, but her eyes were fierce and her jaw was set for the struggle. She wrote articles in a few of the party organs. They were good: engaging, colloquial, funny. CJ read Audrey a few choice excerpts. Finally, in an eight-hundred-word takedown of American Trotskyites, an intellect was described as "dry as sand on a soda cracker." Word for word the same phrase Singapore Sam used about the DA.

"Just like in the movie," Audrey said.

"*She* wrote the screenplay."

For one perfect moment life decided to make sense. CJ had sometimes suspected a female hand behind the language, but this was the solution in full—a communist woman, living in sin in Iowa in 1946. Albert Harris was a rat from the past come to blackmail her, so she had him killed. All the pieces fit. CJ kept searching, but the trail dried up after 1946. Then she remembered why the name Birgit felt familiar. In the 1910 census, Hans Bauer of Collander, Wisconsin had two sons: teenagers Frank and Tom, and a toddler step-daughter—from a mother now deceased. Frank, of course, grew up, fought in the first world war, met Victor Lugo, and got one screen credit for a little picture called *The Jade Ring*. And his baby stepsister?

CJ passed her phone to Audrey.

"Birgit Muntz?"

"From Muntz to Munsey," CJ said. "A lot of Germans took the kraut out of their surnames back then."

This revelation was huge and meaty. There were four or five different articles she needed to write immediately: the intersection of art, gender, political philosophy. CJ was getting dizzy, but Audrey started typing and soon found a Birgit Muntz, living in Arch, Wisconsin—two towns over from Collander. But this woman appeared to be in her seventies.

"Too young," Audrey said.

"It's her daughter."

Old Birgit got knocked up by Frieze (or some other clown) then she moved back up to Wisconsin, had the little bundle, and named it after herself.

"But why is she Muntz instead of Munsey?" Audrey asked.

"Her mom changed it back to stay off some radars."

"And after the war, she figured it was safe to slip the lederhosen back on?"

"I need to go see her."

CJ downed the last of her coffee and stood.

"Right now?" Audrey said.

"If I start now, I'll be there tomorrow."

"Or you could stay with me. Set out in the morning like a civilized human."

"No, it's always best to get an old person early in the day," CJ said. "Come on, I'll drive you home."

Audrey paid and followed CJ out to her car. It was less than ten minutes to Audrey's place. When they got there Audrey asked CJ to walk her to the door then fumbled for her keys a bit before fitting the metal into the lock.

"You got a girlfriend?" Audrey asked.

"No."

"Don't like to be tied down?"

"Something like that."

"You probably got a string of broken hearts longer than that reddit chain you started about the colorized version of *The Big Sleep*."

"How about a kiss goodbye?"

A nip on the chin then the mouth, gently. CJ leaned into this soft little woman. Audrey opened the door and started to pull CJ inside. But CJ didn't cross the threshold.

"Good night," she said.

"You're really going to leave me here? Start driving to Wisconsin?"

"Yes, I am."

"Okay, then."

Audrey closed the door, and CJ walked back to her car. As she reached for the handle, she took a shot to the side of the head that knocked her off her feet.

"Who the hell are you?"

CJ didn't answer. She just looked up at a man, big as her car.

"What were you doing with my girlfriend?" he asked.

"Just checking the woman for ticks."

"You made a big mistake, little man."

"I'm not a little man. I'm a medium-sized woman."

Did he really think she was a man? It was dark and she was wearing a suit. He took her by the lapels and lifted her. CJ heard the click clearly in the still night.

"You need to leave, Scott."

Audrey was clear and confident.

"Do it," Scott said, shaking CJ out in front of him. "Put one right through your little boyfriend. See if it hits me."

"You need to let go of her. And you need to leave."

Scott released his hold and shoved CJ aside. Audrey stood steady with a Colt Commander pointed at the big man.

"Do it," he said. "If you want to kill me, kill me."

"I want you to go home."

They all stood still until Scott turned and walked away.

"You didn't tell me you had a boyfriend," CJ said.

"I don't have a boyfriend. I have a problem. Are you okay?"

"Me? I'm fine."

"Looks like I'm going to Wisconsin with you," Audrey said, getting into the passenger seat.

As CJ started the car, she saw Scott turn and begin running back toward them.

"Reverse. Then take a left at the first intersection," Audrey said.

Scott seemed to be gaining on them as they backed away from the house, but once they hit the turn and started driving forward, Scott faded in the rearview.

"You think he'll burn your place down?"

"He wouldn't do that. Not if I wasn't inside."

Once they made it to the highway, they didn't pass another car for miles—the open seas belonged to them.

"You have work tomorrow?" CJ asked.

"You know what happens if I don't show?"

"Mass hysteria?"

"No one's checked on me in years. I read, watch movies, write snide comments on social media."

"What kind of movies do you like?"

"A lot of trash that'll disappoint you if I say it out loud. I did go through a noir phase in high school."

CJ wasn't crazy about the term "noir phase" but she

liked the low, fluid purr of Audrey's voice.

"I hung around the food court in a cocktail dress and pillbox hat," Audrey said. "They called me the Maltese Mall Tease."

CJ nodded but didn't say anything.

"Birgit Muntz," Audrey continued. "That's a real femme fatale."

And a genuine commie. Not some watered-down humanist who went to a Woody Guthrie concert one time. She was a woman who could write tough-guy dialogue and political treatise, or have a man killed if he turned traitor.

"So what's your theory?" Audrey asked.

"Frank Bauer knew Lugo from their days in the army. Lugo starts directing bad B pictures. They meet for a drink one night—*any monkey could churn out a movie script*. Frank knows his lefty sister can write, so he gets her to bang one out."

"Okay, sure, but I'm talking about the murder."

"An old communist pal comes to Daneville and blackmails her. She has Frieze kill Harris for being a weasel. They set up Murphy, but they also make it so he comes out okay."

"Because Murphy's just a mechanic—an honest working man?"

"Exactly."

"None of that makes any sense," Audrey said.

"Why not?"

"What's the blackmail about?"

"She's a communist. Wouldn't have gone over well in a town like Daneville."

"Daneville was just a place to keep the trunk and a few spare frocks. Things get bad, they just find a cheap room in another little town."

"No, that's—"

"And you're trying to tell me that the film she wrote under her brother's name just happens to give them the right alibi at the right time?"

CJ grew frustrated, then angry, but Audrey was right.

"Okay. No blackmail," CJ said. "Munsey, Frieze, and Harris knew each other from their commie days. Frieze went over to Harris's room to talk over the old times."

"Toss around a few dialectics and sing 'The Internationale'?"

"So they get a little drunk, Harris says something ugly, Frieze strangles him."

"No, Frieze went over there to kill Harris. Remember how he's got an alibi set up, even did a little routine with a sawbuck at the box office so they'd remember him. It was premeditated. Frieze had a reason."

CJ looked over at Audrey. Was it really so surprising that an archivist would have a head on her shoulders?

"Let's see what the daughter knows," CJ said.

They glided into Illinois, past a seventy-foot grain silo and road signs promising salvation and Dr. Pepper.

"You know why I laughed when I first saw you?" Audrey asked.

"Why?"

"Your eyes. They're intense. Like you're trying to intimidate a wild animal."

"And that's why you laughed?"

"When we go see this old bird, you probably want to get your face under control."

Of course, this wasn't the first time CJ had been told that her eyes were fierce and off-putting. They also served as a kind of beacon for a certain type of lost girl.

"Are my eyes okay now?" CJ looked over at Audrey.

"They're gorgeous."

CJ looked back at the road.

"We're ahead of schedule. There's campgrounds in about twenty miles. We can pull in and get some sleep before going to see the lady."

"I'm not sleeping in a car," Audrey said.

"I can't afford a motel."

"I can."

Thirty-eight miles from Arch, Wisconsin, they found a Super 8. CJ knew it was a mistake to have brought Audrey, and the next mistake was going to be even bigger. She was about to cede a bit of herself in a cheap room just when she could least afford it. A woman like this always took something from you. When it was just a T-shirt or an out-of-print DVD, you were getting off easy.

* * *

Audrey was still in bed at eight the next morning. A fitful sleeper, she tossed and mumbled—*can't hear*. But there was time. The best hour to hit an old person was between ten and eleven. Once you were in their house, it was tough for them to tell you to leave; and once you got them talking, they often spilled the whole story from title to credits. If you pressed even more, you could find yourself in the attic sorting through treasure.

CJ got a cup of coffee and the local paper. A high school girl working at Burger King had killed the owner of the franchise. Ten-to-one the boss man had it coming. By the time CJ got back to the room, Audrey was up and ready to go.

Birgit Muntz was a tall woman who went by Bonnie. She greeted them warily, but after a few awkward moments, she invited them in and even set out a few Lorna Doones on the coffee table. The home was clean and sparsely decorated, but there was an unwholesome smell coming from the carpet.

"We believe that your mother created one of the greatest films of all time," CJ said.

"My Uncle Frank you mean? He was the one in movies."

"No, your mother, Birgit Munsey. The world should know more about her."

Bonnie broke a cookie in half but left both the pieces on the tray.

"You're talking about that little—jade picture?" she asked.

"*The Jade Ring*, yes, ma'am."

"Yeah. Mom wrote that. You think it's one of the greatest movies ever made?"

"I believe it with all my soul."

"It's no *Gone with the Wind*."

CJ took a very deep breath and clutched the armrest tight.

"But she had to use your uncle as a front because she was a communist. Is that right?"

"Who was a communist?"

"In the '30s, your mother—"

"Oh, she joined the organizations, wrote some—tracts, screeds, whatever you call them. But that's not who she was."

"Who was she?"

Bonnie Muntz smiled and shrugged.

"I guess it can't hurt to tell now," she said. "And even if it does, she deserves a little pain. She drove my dad away."

"Who was your dad?"

"The husband of my mom," she said—snappy answer to a stupid question.

"What was his name?"

"Daniel Frieze."

"But they weren't married."

"Excuse me—yes, they were. Married over there. But when they came back to America, it was better that they had different names."

"Why?"

"She was spying."

"For who?"

"The Germans."

"The—Germans?"

No, this made no sense.

"So she was a Nazi?" Audrey asked.

"And she wasn't a very good mother, either." Bonnie shook her head. "She met Dad in Berlin in 1933. She was in Europe, working for a company that sold fancy jackets. He was playing trombone in a dance band. Both of them native-born Americans who thought there was something to this Third Reich. They fell for each other, too. The Nazis thought they might be more useful back in the states. Dad got them to send regular cash."

"For infiltrating the United States Communist Party?"

"Take the temperature over here." Bonnie grew more comfortable, even a little slick as she told the story. "Turned out Dad wasn't much of an actor. Put him in a room with those queer ducks, he'd just get too angry, threaten to throw someone out a window. But Mom could keep it cool. I'll give her that much."

"So the woman who wrote *The Jade Ring* was a fascist," Audrey said.

This was just a game to her, a funny story told by an entertaining old lady. But Audrey was wrong. Birgit Munsey was a triple agent, working the Nazis *for* the reds. You couldn't write like she did while working for the wrong team.

"She mellowed over time," Bonnie continued. "But, you know, certain politicians, businessmen would get her going. When Rosenstein bought up all the A&Ps. 'Swell, we get to buy all our bread from that *Rosenstein* now.'"

The old woman was doing a voice. In structure and cadence it resembled the tart responses Ramona spat out at the slow-witted cop. Bonnie pushed the plate of cookies to the center of the table.

"I'm not saying it's right," she said, "but, you have to admit, there's something there."

"Something where?"

"When you have a tiny group of people who control so much of the world, the money. Is *that* right?"

"Did your mother write anything else?" Audrey asked.

"She was always writing—articles, stories. Uncle Frank got her some radio work for a while."

"Radio work?"

"She'd send pages to one of those men who yells at you on the AM dial. They don't just make it up as they go along."

"This is ridiculous," CJ said. "None of this is true."

"You're calling me a liar?"

"I'm calling you—a liar."

"Get out of my house."

Bonnie wasn't afraid of a woman in a double-breasted suit.

"I want to see what she wrote, what she left behind. It's here—in the house."

"I'm calling the police."

Bonnie lifted the receiver of an old landline. CJ took one stride toward her, but Audrey stepped in and ran a hand up her shoulder.

"Come on. Let's go."

CJ could easily yank the phone away and tie this hag to a chair. Birgit Munsey deserved to have her memory celebrated. Instead, she'd been betrayed by a daughter gone fash. All the proof was in this house—papers, letters, unfinished novels, essays, screenplays. But Audrey's touch, still with the power of last night's intimacy, eased her to the door.

Ten minutes later they were back on the highway.

"This is some story," Audrey said. "You got Nazis, you got movie people, you got shortbread cookies in Wisconsin."

Audrey settled into the passenger seat—flip and cruel. She was nothing but a petty, hateful civil servant.

"There's no Nazis," CJ said. "Bonnie is a racist old woman being strange. Birgit Munsey was the genuine article."

"I've known a lot of racist old women. None of them make up Nazi parents."

"Birgit Munsey was a communist, a radical—"

"You're just going to ignore the parts you don't like?"

"I'm going to ignore what doesn't make sense. That's called logic."

"If you're not going to tell it right, I will."

"What do you mean?"

"Put a noun in front of a verb, pretty soon you have an article."

CJ stopped the car and pulled onto the shoulder.

"You can't write about this."

"Maybe I can dig a little on the German side. I know a few archivists over in Europe, and—"

"No, there is no German side. Get that through your head."

"Albert Harris found out who they really were. They lured him out to Iowa—"

"Shut up. You'd never even seen *The Jade Ring* until last night."

"It doesn't belong to you just because you've cared about it the longest."

Audrey got out of the car. What was she going to do, walk back to town? CJ followed, slamming the door behind them.

"Anyway, the story isn't even about the movie," Audrey said. "It's about a couple of Nazis who—"

"No, *Jade* is the whole point."

"One cheap B movie? Bad production values, so-so dialogue, no real—"

"How would you know what a good movie is?"

"*Jade* was made to kill ninety minutes. It's not *Double Indemnity* or *Maltese Falcon* or—"

"Get the hell out of my face with *Falcon*. *Falcon* has so many problems. First of all—"

"I don't need a lecture. And I don't need to see *Jade* two hundred times to know it's trash."

CJ didn't remember when she'd grabbed Audrey by the wrists, but when the little archivist tried to pull free, CJ shoved her sideways and her head slammed hard against the side of the car. CJ charged at her as Audrey rolled onto her side, pulled her gun, and fired once.

CJ fell into the dirt. The bullet had ripped clean through her jacket, her shirt. She felt the wetness just under the ribcage. The car started and backed up, passing just inches from her head. Then it turned away and drove off. CJ managed to sit up, then stand and walk along the side of the highway.

She had no car, and the pain flared all along the left side of her body. Her steps became uneven, but there were things that hurt a lot worse than taking a bullet to the gut. In Bonnie Muntz's home, she'd find everything she needed.

Preston Lang is a Toronto-based writer. He's written dozens of stories and at least three novels.

The Bunker Girl

By Alec Cizak

Gilbert's mother sat on the couch with him. She wore her usual baggy, sky blue muumuu and a clear shower cap. They'd been watching *Family Feud* when the old-fashioned flip model in Gilbert's pocket chirped like a parakeet. He palmed it and answered. As Seth Short gave him instructions, Gilbert's mother tapped his elbow, repeated, "Where'd you get that?" She pointed at the cell. Would not let Gilbert focus on the conversation with Seth. He said, "Hold up, boss," and put his hand over the mic.

"You know I can't multitask," he said to his mother.

"I want to know where you got that."

Gilbert stood and started for the front door. His mother said, "You ain't working for them rednecks again, are you?"

He stepped onto the stoop outside and slammed the door. That would let her know to mind her own business. "I'm back," he said into the phone.

"Stink," said Seth, "how'd you like to drive a car to

Chicago for me?"

Seth lived in a two-story shithole near Lublin. What lawn remained hadn't been mowed in a quarter century. Rot plagued the house's cedar walls. Termites, Gilbert assumed. Smoke lolled over the edges of a leaning chimney. Seth lumbered like Lurch, from the Addams Family. He hated jokes about his ungodly height. He walked Gilbert around to the side. Slipped him the keys to a maroon Honda Civic. Nothing flashy, nothing to catch the beady eyes of Lake County or Chitown pigs. He punched an address into the car's GPS and said, "You ask for Diego when you get there. He'll be expecting you." He explained how to hide the package in the trunk, underneath the factory-provided spare tire and flimsy jack. "Stink," he said, "I'm glad you're with us again." He waved a finger in his face. "I want New Stink on this job, not Old Stink, you dig?"

Gilbert told him he could count on him. Promised he wouldn't fuck things up. Seth sent him on his own. A relief. Gilbert'd gotten in good with Seth once more by accompanying Crank Baxter on a hit the previous week. A nasty task. Hadn't slept well since. Crank had picked him up in a rusted Ford Courier. It coughed and choked as he urged it to seventy miles an hour. They pulled into Haggard after midnight. Parked across from the underground bunker at the water plant. Crank Baxter resembled a World War II tank. Squat, sturdy frame built in the mills in Gary. He stalked the bunker's green haze hunched over; a cat poised to kill. Shoved his way through clusters of junkies. He grabbed people by their throats, lifted them off the ground, and Darth Vader'd them about a guy named Bobby Arnold.

A young woman with honey-brown hair directed them to a concrete lip just above the sewage ducts. Rodents nipped at Bobby Arnold's toes as he scrunched himself inside the narrow space. Must have figured it an easier fate than dealing with Crank Baxter. Mud stained his jeans and trendy Johnny Cash T-shirt, the one with the Man in Black showing the camera his middle finger.

Crank dragged him through the crowd. The junkies cussed, threatened to kick his ass. "Help me get this piece of shit to the surface," he said to Gilbert. For a junkie, Bobby Arnold looked healthy. Overweight, but youthful, shiny skin. Probably new to the scene. Gilbert struggled to keep his balance as he pushed Bobby's feet through the steel-rimmed portal leading to the sane world. Crank hoisted him from above, his monster hands clutching the junkie's shoulders. As Gilbert climbed the iron rungs to the street, Crank Baxter thwacked Bobby Arnold in the side of his neck. The junkie collapsed. Crank dragged him by his ankle to the truck. "Let's go, Stink," he said. Gilbert wished he had the balls to correct the gangsters, tell them nobody needed to call him Stinky anymore. His underarms and unwashed Haynes begged to differ. He helped Crank chuck the junkie onto the bed of the pickup. Two five-gallon gas cannisters and several coils of chains had been secured behind the cab.

As they bounced and slid over a gravel road near Pawpaw Grove, Gilbert asked, "What's the deal?"

Crank stared at him for a moment. "Bobby's been busted seven times now and never once been tossed over the wall."

Gilbert ceased thinking of Bobby Arnold as a junkie. Junkies deserved sympathy. But rats? They required swift execution.

"Going to take him for a ride." Crank steered the Ford onto a wide, dirt path at Pawpaw Hollow. He brought the truck to a halt among cedars and birch trees. "Let's get the snitch prepped for his last meal." He clarified: "Bobby's going to feast on twigs and pebbles before meeting his maker."

They secured the rat's legs with the chains and attached the other ends to a hitch on the tail of the truck. Bobby stirred as they set him on the ground. "Why not just shoot him?" said Gilbert.

"Boy needs to think about his mistakes as he's dying." Crank walked back to the cab.

Bobby Arnold opened his eyes. He held his pudgy hands out to Gilbert. Baby hands. "Please, buddy..."

"Stink!" Crank honked the horn twice.

The engine growled. An impatient predator. Crank jammed his left foot onto the brake pedal and fed the engine gas with his right. The hood rattled. Crank released the brake and the truck coughed before taking off.

Not even the chorus of the wind harmonizing with the Ford's raspy protests drowned the horrid sounds of Bobby Arnold's shrieks. Fate must have blessed him, snapped his neck, early in the ride. Gilbert glanced at his sideview mirror. The rat's limp body trampolined off the earth like a fish reeled in across a lake. The image visited him any time he caught a moment's sleep the following days.

Crank slowed and stopped the truck in a clearing. He pointed at a parked violet Geo. "Our chariot home." He directed Gilbert to reach under his seat. Said he'd find two sets of work gloves. "This is going to be messy."

The road repurposed Bobby Arnold into a sopping crimson slab. As they heaved the dead rat onto the bed of the truck, his skeleton collapsed. Multiple bones must have splintered or broken. Crank instructed Gilbert to climb over the fleshy glob and retrieve the cannisters of gasoline. Gilbert handed them to him. "Jump down, now," said Crank. He picked up one of the containers and splashed the corpse and the truck. He nodded to the other cannister. "Let's go, Stink. This heap ain't going to bathe itself."

Gilbert unscrewed the lid. The container felt heavier as he doused the front end of the truck. He circled the vehicle several times. The air wobbled like a movie flashback, reeked of benzene. Crank threw his cannister onto the bed and told Gilbert to do the same. He produced a Zippo with a copper Grim Reaper etched into the side of it. "Stand back, Stink." He lit the Reaper and aimed it at the Ford. Sparks jumped until a small fire danced where the Zippo landed. The flames mated with the fuel. A vicious gust preceded a blaze encompassing the truck and the rat.

Crank smacked Gilbert in the chest with the back of his hand. "Let's go, Stink." He threw a set of keys at him and walked toward the Geo. "You drive this time, buddy."

* * *

A week later, Gilbert exited the Dan Ryan Express at 35th and crawled through cramped traffic to Union. The GPS directed him to a two-story brick building on the corner. A liquor store occupied the first floor. Men on the sidewalk asked for spare change from anyone entering or leaving the booze shop. Women in painted-on skirts chirped at him, asked if he needed some pussy. One woman, could not have been older than sixteen, offered to suck his dick. He patted his pockets, pretended he had no cash. He found the entryway leading to the apartments. On a keypad with scratched off numbers, he dialed the number Seth gave him. A man on the other end asked what the hell he wanted. "Name's Gilbert," he said. "I'm here to see Diego." The door buzzed and he ascended a set of marble stairs riddled with cracks. At the top of the steps, a man wider than Gilbert, dressed in safari shorts and a wine-red Bermuda shirt, chomped a cigar. His snow-white eyebrows and hair suggested he had a decade on Gilbert.

In a polite tone, he said, "Please raise your arms." He patted down Gilbert with one hand. A lazy inspection. "It's cool," he said. "Seth tells me you're old school."

Gilbert pointed to the gray patch of hair arcing over his left ear. "Been around a while, amigo."

"Sí, ese." The man appeared neither amused nor impressed. He directed him into a small room with torn furniture and a flat screen television mounted in the window. He rested his cigar across the top of a Coke can. From under a couch suitable for a museum—the ornate, wooden arms and legs carved to resemble the feet and claws of an unidentified animal—the man produced a briefcase with a broken combination lock. He opened it and pointed to a collection of plastic baggies stuffed with pills.

After closing the briefcase, the man stepped aside. "All yours."

Gilbert did so and left the apartment. He recognized several of the pills—Vikes, Oxy, and Fen, ready to be crushed and snorted or shot into the arms of Lake County's living dead. He never plugged dope. Considered it a waste. Better to pop a pill, let the body warm to the chemical seasoning. A couple of Vikes, he could haunt a bar and not make a fool of himself in front of women. Then again, he hadn't gone out in years. He preferred to sit on the couch in his mother's house and veg to late night television.

He roamed the liquor store. Pulled an RC from a cooler near the emergency exit. As he approached the counter, he noticed a young woman in cut-off shorts. Ass cheeks peeking out the bottom. Pink halter top. No bra. Honey-brown hair. His attention volleyed between her and the clerk as he paid for the soda. He told the clerk to keep the change.

He ignored the men outside asking for money, the hookers ogling him, as though he owed them attention. The young woman in cutoffs trailed him to the rental. He stopped and said, "Excuse me?"

"I know you." She placed her knuckles on her hips. A nearby streetlamp, one of the few working on the block, washed out her eyes. "Met you in the bunker, in Haggard."

He ducked into a shadow.

"Last week," she said, "you barged through looking for that fat ugly snitch, Bobby Arnold."

"No idea what you're talking about."

She waved her hand. "Oh, don't worry none. Nobody's going to miss that fucking skinhead."

"I got to go." Gilbert started for the driver's side.

"Back to Haggard?"

Gilbert pressed the button on the keychain to open the door.

"Think I could get a ride?" The young woman tilted her head. "Really," she said, "I promise I won't tell no one you clipped the snitch."

"Who said I did?"

The young woman stepped toward the passenger-side door and fiddled with the handle. "Come on, man," she said. "I don't get a ride, I'm going to have to spend the night with a creep. You know how dudes from Chicago are. Total douchebags."

Gilbert's lungs deflated. He'd yet to shake the moronic belief that doing favors for women led to sex. Sex he wouldn't pay for in the most overt, socially unacceptable manner. He imagined the young woman in lingerie, after a shower and a makeover. She'd look good. What had she been doing in the bunker? No blemishes on her arms or legs from plugging dope. Did she pop pills? He could buy some from Seth and ask the young woman to chill with him. "Hop on in." He clicked the trunk button on the keychain and wedged the briefcase between the spare tire and first aid kit.

As Chicago's obscene skyscrapers diminished in the rearview, the young woman unloaded biographical details. Whether she told the truth, Gilbert didn't care. She claimed a redneck shot her ex-boyfriend in the Van & Strack parking lot. Cops wanted to pin it on her. Not enough evidence. She laid low in the bunker to be safe. "Never know when the pigs might decide to take a closer look." Gilbert asked if the man's death had been her fault. She changed the subject. "Got a line to Classy Companions."

"What's that?"

"Escort service."

"Oh."

"I won't be selling my pussy, per se. Just showing it to douchebags while they tug themselves." She stared out her window. "I know, it's kind of gross. But I won't cross that line. I won't take money to let a man inside me."

"You shouldn't," said Gilbert. "I mean, I'm not judging. I just think...You look like you have more respect for yourself, you know?" His mother would have laughed. She'd put her foot down a year ago, told him to stop bringing hookers to his bedroom.

A purple and gray sky loitered over the dead mills in Gary. The young woman mumbled. Something like, "Yeah, sure."

Gilbert took the first exit to Haggard. He needed to gas up the rental and grab something sweet for his belly. He pulled into the Shell station overlooking I-65 like a parent at a playground. He asked the young woman if she needed anything. She said no. Very considerate of her. "Sit tight," he said. He swiped his mother's credit card at the pump and fed the tank. He greeted a posse of homeless cats he'd gotten to know in recent months. They stood by the door, opening it for customers coming and going, hoping for charity. "Get you on my way out," he said to them. He perused the snack aisle, his mouth watering at the shelf of Hostess sugar bombs. He nabbed a cherry pie and stood in line. He used his own cash. On his way back to the car, he dropped three quarters in the smudged, free hand of the man holding the door. The guy sneered. "It's all I got," said Gilbert.

Guilt from not helping the homeless man buy a four-course meal and whatever poison put him on the street evaporated when he returned to the rental. The woman had taken off. Jesus, he should have known better. Good-looking twenty-something, even if she dwelled in the bunker, what the hell would she want with a rotting fifty-three-year-old? He grinned at himself in the rearview as he settled in the car. Half his teeth, missing. Blackened, chipped, crooked. A hillbilly Red Foxx. "Loser," he said to himself. He took off and cruised to Seth's place. The big man sat at a crumbling picnic table out front. Flaking paint suggested the benches had once been canary and the table itself, burnt orange. Probably stolen from the old Haggard public swimming pool. Gilbert parked and meandered to the table, wiping pie crumbs off the corners of his mouth. Seth picked up the barrel of a black revolver he'd disassembled and peered through it. "What's the word, Stink?"

Gilbert clicked the keychain and popped the trunk. "No issues." He walked with Seth to the car. Seth arrived a second earlier. His eyes rummaged the trunk.

"Johnnies pulled you over," he said, "looks like you'd a had nothing to worry about."

Gilbert's throat dried. The young woman had robbed him. He'd failed to hide the dope the way Seth instructed. He'd fucked up. Again. He marched around to the driver's side, bent down to examine several buttons near the emergency brake. "Shit..."

"Where's my product, Stink?" Impatience colored Seth's voice.

The young woman had found the button for the trunk, no doubt took a peek, and snatched the briefcase. He inhaled. Closed his eyes. "I guess...there was an issue."

Seth slammed the trunk and circled the car. "How's that?"

"I gave a ride..."

Pointing at him with the detached gun barrel, Seth said, "Changed my mind, Stink. Not in the mood to hear the story. Get me my pills or get your affairs in order.

I'm tired of giving you second chances."

Technically, he'd only given him *two* second chances. Gilbert stuffed himself into the car and started it up without saying anything. Seth approached the driver's side and tapped the window with the gun barrel. Gilbert rolled it down. The big man leaned in and said, "Got one hour, Stink. Beyond that, I'm sending Crank Baxter your way. You know how that's going to turn out, don't you?"

* * *

Gilbert's mother dubbed Seth Short The Overseer. Said he'd have taken delight in whipping returned runaways back in the day. Gilbert considered these things as he climbed down the rusted rungs to the bunker at the water plant. Usual litter of junkies on the narrow lip beside the flowing sewage. They'd slumped against the concrete wall, huddled, on the nod. *Shit.* Common sense told him he'd retrieve nothing. Perhaps he could offer up the young woman as a sacrifice to Seth.

"Anybody seen..." He'd never thought to ask her name. Or did she tell him and he'd forgotten? Yes, yes. She said it once. Something fancy, something foreign sounding, like she belonged in a Hans Christian Andersen story. A junkie in a striped shirt and torn blue jeans raised his head. He squinted, as though staring into the sun.

"Sup, dawg?"

"I'm looking for a girl," said Gilbert. "Short shorts, pink halter top, dusty brown hair, possibly blonde, I'm not good with colors."

"Think you mean Cym." The junkie used his bulbous

forehead to point down the line. "She's earned a spot with Mitch."

"Mitch Polk?" said Gilbert.

The junkie said, "Last names are still a thing in the world upstairs?"

Gilbert thanked him and walked into the tunnel. Mitch Polk had been a runner for Seth. Gilbert heard he'd died at some point. Overdosed. Or Seth had him eighty-sixed. Depended on who told the story. The bunker hid a lot of Haggard's dirt. His eyes adjusted to the dim and he spotted the young woman's legs, draped over another man in filthy jeans. "Hey," he said when he reached her.

The young woman took her time facing him.

"What'd you do with it?" he said.

The man she'd wrapped herself around forced his chin higher. "Who are you?"

"Mitch?"

"Stink?"

"Nobody calls me that no more." He returned his attention to the young woman. "I need the shit you peeled."

"No idea what you're talking about." The young woman flashed her teeth. So white they glowed in the dark. A flirtatious smile. No doubt certain she could tease her way out of trouble.

"Ain't here to bullshit," said Gilbert. "I just need that shit back."

Mitch must have thought Gilbert couldn't hear him. "He talking about the dope?"

The young woman played dumb.

"Oh, bro," said Mitch, "that shit's long gone." He waved his hand back and forth. "Everybody got some."

He clutched the brick wall to help him get to his feet. "And thank you, if you're the donor."

Gilbert's fingers clasped the junkie's clammy throat. "You understand Seth Short's going to turn your ass inside-out, right?"

Mitch laughed. "Wouldn't be the first time."

"Dude," said the young woman, "the shit's gone. Just deal with it."

Gilbert released Mitch, let him drop to his knees to catch his breath. To the young woman, he said, "You familiar with karma?"

"That's superstitious shit for people who can't handle reality."

"It's very real," said Gilbert.

The young woman shrugged.

The bunker's emerald glow tapered. Gilbert knew he could pick her up, throttle her, throw her into the river of sewage. Wouldn't matter. He'd still have to go to Seth empty. Still have to take his lumps. "Okay," he said to the young woman. "See you on the other side."

He climbed out of the bunker and drove to the Family Express on Seventh Street. He used his mother's credit card to buy a bottle of Night Train and sat in the rental downing it. Before putting the Honda into gear and heading toward Seth's, toward whatever harsh judgment The Overseer had in store for him, he called his mother on the disposable flip phone. "Hey," he said. "Just wanted to thank you." She asked what the hell had gotten into him. "You jet through life," he said to her, "someone right next to you, telling you what you need to hear, and you don't listen until it's too late."

"Well, yeah..." Her sarcasm? *Music.*

"I got to go, Mom." He hung up and coasted onto

Seventh Street. He fired up the rental's satellite radio. Found a station playing songs from the nineties. All that grunge crap he couldn't stand, taking him back to his days as a young man, when he still believed his future lay in Chicago and beyond. When he still believed he would not be buried in the same town he'd been born in.

Alec Cizak is a writer and filmmaker from Indiana. His recent books include Down on the Street, Breaking Glass, Lake County Incidents, *and* Cool It Down. *He is also the editor of the digest magazine* Pulp Modern.

Smokey and Magic Mike v. Progress

By Jay Butkowski

Smokey wiped down a rocks glass and watched the stranger with curiosity as he parked a silver Lexus SUV and entered the bar. He didn't look like their usual clientele—madras shirt under a brown corduroy blazer and tucked into a pair of regular fit Dockers. Brown leather loafers with no socks and thick, pomaded hair. Smokey could smell the stink of Drakkar Noir from the other side of the room, even over the dank, earthy richness of some of their best-selling merchandise.

Not the kind of guy Smokey was used to seeing in their establishment, and certainly not in the middle of the afternoon.

Normally, they'd have bikers in and out of here—patched leather dudes, easy riders who'd stop by for a beer and a toke before heading further upstate. Sometimes, they'd have a couple old heads like Smokey himself stop in, decked out in their Birks and knitted ponchos and beaded hair, looking to kill some brain cells and relive the glory days. Occasionally, they'd get a gaggle of college kids who were looking to track down El Dorado and could rarely handle their shit.

This preppy youngster was early for the happy hour blitz and didn't fit into any of those groups. He looked like a fish out of water to ol' Smokey: completely out of his element.

"Can I help you, friend?"

"That depends," said the stranger. "Is this the famous Smokey and Mike's Roadside Saloon, BBQ Pit, and Head Shop?"

"You with the IRS?"

"No, sir!"

"DEA?"

The stranger laughed. "No, I swear, I'm not with the government! Just out here, looking for a legend."

Smokey stroked his long gray beard and scratched his paunchy belly, weighing the flattery. He didn't feel particularly legendary.

"Well, if you ain't five-oh, I guess you're in the right place."

"So then, you're...?"

"Smokey D. Bear, at your service." Smokey wiped a big, bear paw of a hand on his pants leg and extended it over the bartop. The stranger took it and pumped vigorously.

"Oh, wow, this is an honor, sir. David Simpkins. Is your partner, Mike, around too?"

Smokey gestured a thumb over his shoulder. "He's around back. He's more grower, and I'm more shower, if you get my meaning. He runs the back-of-the-house operations, and leaves customer service to me."

"This place is amazing." Simpkins gawked. "How long have you guys been here?"

"Since Woodstock. Me, Mike, and a couple of pretty

young ladies hopped into a VW minibus, and took off from Dayton, Ohio for the best three days and fifty-two years of my life. After the festival, the ladies took a Greyhound back home, and me and Mike, well, we stayed and set up shop here."

"I've heard from people that you guys grow some of the best weed on the planet," said the preppy.

"That's all Mike," said Smokey. "We don't call him Magic for nuthin'. Guy's got the greenest thumb I've ever seen. Doesn't hurt that we've got all of nature's splendor helping us out, too."

"Yeah, I could barely find the place."

"We kind of like it like that," said Smokey. "Not so many cell towers up in the mountains, and the service is even worse in the valley. Helps keep away the riff-raff."

"The cops don't give you guys a hard time?"

"You're talking about a different kind of smokey now, friend." The old timer removed his bifocals and wiped off the smudges with the bottom of his tie-dyed Dancing Bears T-shirt. "Yeah, the local authorities and us, we got an understanding here. There was one guy, few years back, who was a bit of a hard ass, bad for business, y'know? But the rest just leave us be. Figure, with the Oxy, and the crank, and all that shit out there these days, they got their hands full and don't need to be banging down the doors of a couple old potheads."

"Is it true you guys are thanked in the liner notes of Willie Nelson's *Greatest Hits* album?"

"Willie's a pal. Usually stops by when he's in town."

"And you guys partied with Wu Tang once too, right?"

"Hey man, they ain't nuthin' to fuck with." Smokey was getting a little bit annoyed at the younger man's exuberance. "You going to buy something?"

"Maybe, if the price is right. What would you say you and Mike clear in a year of running this fine establishment? Financially speaking," asked Simpkins, the facade of fanboy excitement slipping away.

"Who exactly did you say you were with?" asked Smokey.

A few moments later, the serene Hudson Valley setting outside Smokey and Mike's Roadside was disrupted, as the door was flung open with a loud and reverberating *thwack*, and David Simpkins of ACG CanniBusiness Associates, LLC, was tossed out into the gravel parking lot.

"Get the fuck out of here!" roared Smokey, emerging from the darkened portal.

"You're making a big mistake!" sniveled Simpkins.

Mike came running from around the other side of the building, tall, gaunt, and grim in a black leather cowboy hat and black tank top. "Smoke, what the fuck is going on?"

"This pencil-dick is trying to buy us out!"

"Slow down," said Mike.

"You guys are fossils!" shouted Simpkins, a thin line of blood tracking from nostril to lip from when Smokey had decked him in the bar before tossing him into the parking lot. "I don't even know how you survived this long, but in case you haven't heard, weed is legal now, assholes, and it's big business! And you either adapt, or you die."

"You sunuva..." Smokey kicked at the younger man but Mike restrained him.

Simpkins took the opportunity to scramble to his feet and dust himself off. He indignantly spat at the older men, a mix of saliva and nose-blood.

"Thing is, I don't even have to buy you out, dipshit. I was trying to do this the nice way—the polite way, the respectful way. I figured you had connections, maybe you're marketable. But then you had to go and hit me. It's your funeral. I'll sue your ass, and when I'm done with that, we'll flood this valley with cheaper, legal weed, put you guys right out of business. You fucked with the wrong hombre, asshole! Shit, maybe I'll even call it Smokey's Special, really fuck with your client base."

Mike was the quieter, cooler head of the two, but even he had a breaking point, and professional pride demanded swift retribution. Quicker than a cobra strike, he pulled a big-ass handgun, tucked neatly into the back waistband of his jeans. He fired a single round straight through the tinted back windows of the parked Lexus, the boom of the gunshot shattering safety glass and sending nearby birds into flight. He swung the gun back around and pointed it at Simpkins, who dropped to his knees and wet himself.

In between sobs, pleas, and prayers, Simpkins gurgled, "I thought...you guys were just a couple harmless...hippies..."

"Nah, man, we're businessmen," said Smokey. He savagely kicked Simpkins in the stomach, doubling him over. "And you threatened our bottom line, friend."

Smokey and Mike each grabbed under an armpit and hoisted the vanquished corporate raider back to his feet. They each took a turn, alternating between hitting the younger man or holding him up to be hit. As they pressed him against the side of the Lexus, a rusted-out police cruiser came rolling up the road.

"Smokey, Mike, what in the H-E-double-L is going on out here," asked the officer from inside the car.

"Just teaching young Master Simpkins a lesson," said Smokey, adding, "in business ethics."

"Well, wouldya keep it down?" asked the officer. "Your G-D neighbors called in a noise complaint over that gunshot."

"Aye Aye, Captain." Smokey faux-saluted.

The officer continued down the road, and the beating continued.

* * *

David Simpkins sat on his expensive leather sofa, in his luxury Jersey City apartment, holding a bag of frozen peas to his swollen and bruised face. It was dark, and late, and his head was pounding, but however bad he felt, he was sure he looked even worse.

He got up and peered into a mirror by the front entrance. Blood caked under his nose and onto his torn shirt collar. His right eye was an egg; his lip busted and split. He touched thumb and forefinger to a front tooth, and he could swear it felt loose.

"Fucking psychos," he muttered. "And what was with that fucking useless cop?"

This was his third strike in a month up in Hudson Valley, and though the other old timers hadn't devolved into violence, none took kindly to his offer either.

"Buncha goddamned hillbillies," he said to himself.

You can't fight progress, he thought, even as he winced and clutched his bruised ribs that proved otherwise.

Jay Butkowski is a writer of crime fiction and an eater of tacos who lives in New Jersey. His short stories have appeared in various online and print publications, including Shotgun Honey, Yellow Mama, All Due Respect, *and* Vautrin. *He is the Managing Editor and one of the co-founders of Rock and a Hard Place Press, an independent publisher of noir chronicling "bad decisions and desperate people" in short and longer format fiction, as well as in the flagship* Rock and a Hard Place Magazine. *He's also a father of twins, a doting fiancé, and a middling pancake chef.*

BOOKS

On the following pages are a few
more great titles from the
Down & Out Books publishing family.

For a complete list of books and to
sign up for our newsletter,
go to DownAndOutBooks.com.

Person Unknown
Michael Penncavage

All Due Respect, an imprint of
Down & Out Books
October 2021
978-1-64396-223-8

Life is going great for Steve Harrison. Only thirty-five years old, he's already a Senior Vice President for a major financial firm. He's admired by his co-workers, his friends, his wife—and his mistress. There's nothing he can't handle. The world, as they say, is his oyster.

And all of that is about to change…

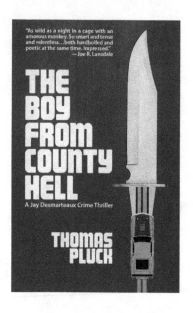

The Boy from County Hell
A Jay Desmarteaux Crime Thriller
Thomas Pluck

Down & Out Books
November 2021
978-1-64396-234-4

Jay Desmarteaux raised a whole lot of hell after he was released from prison after 25 years for the murder of a rapist bully at his school.

Now he's on the run in his home state of Louisiana, and traces his roots to an evil family tree that's grown large and lush, watered with the blood of the innocent.

A tree that needs chopping down.

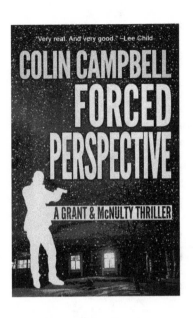

Forced Perspective
A Grant & McNulty Thriller
Colin Campbell

Down & Out Books
December 2021
978-1-64396-241-2

Jim Grant enlists Vince McNulty's help to invite criminals to audition as movie extras. The plan is almost derailed when McNulty and Grant protect a girl from an angry biker but the plan is successful. Mostly.

Except the sting is a dry run for the main person Grant wants to arrest; a crime lord movie buff in Loveland, Colorado. A sting that won't be nearly as successful.

Sharp Knives and Loud Guns
The Paignton Noir Case Files
Tom Leins

All Due Respect, an imprint of
Down & Out Books
December 2021
978-1-64396-239-9

This brand-new collection of Paignton Noir Case Files is from cult crime writer Tom Leins, featuring the novelettes Slug Bait, Smut Loop and Sweating Blood.

In these violent misadventures private investigator Joe Rey is forced to confront his dark past—if he still wants to have a future. Things are about to get very bloody, very quickly…